WYOMING'S MOST ELIGIBLE BACHELORS

1. Chad ~~Randall~~
2. Pete ~~Randall~~
3. Brett ~~Randall~~
4. Jake ~~Randall~~
5. *Griffin Randall*

Cons	Pros
hard-hearted	good-lookin'
mule-headed	hot-blooded
love 'em & leave 'em	rough & ready

No

D0964925

Dear Reader,

When I first thought of doing a series about a family of brothers on a ranch in Wyoming, I had no idea how much those four men would come to mean to me. I fell in love with them! Jake, the protective oldest brother, Pete, a hardheaded, determined man, Brett, lighthearted and loving, and Chad, the baby, who wanted to prove himself but idolized Jake—they became my ideal men. Yes, they are all stubborn and demanding, but they love each other. And they each secretly wanted a woman to share their lives.

Best of all, they love children, and macho though they are, they think nothing of changing diapers. My kind of heroes!

Given the opportunity to revisit the Randall ranch, I couldn't resist. So here's the last of the Randalls, Griffin, a Chicago cowboy, alone and ignorant of the ways of a family like the Randalls. But blood is thicker than water, and Griff discovers he has more in common with these Wyoming Randalls than he'd thought.

I hope you enjoy visiting the Randalls once again.

Judy Christenberry

⑤

COWBOY COME HOME

JUDY CHRISTENBERRY

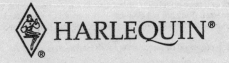

HARLEQUIN®

TORONTO • NEW YORK • LONDON
AMSTERDAM • PARIS • SYDNEY • HAMBURG
STOCKHOLM • ATHENS • TOKYO • MILAN • MADRID
PRAGUE • WARSAW • BUDAPEST • AUCKLAND

To my niece,
Heather Hughes, who loves reading and
cowboys as much as me.
Thanks for all the encouragement, Heather.

ISBN 0-373-16744-X

COWBOY COME HOME

Copyright © 1998 by Judy Christenberry.

Chapter One

"Jake Randall, B.J. said to tell you you're in big trouble!" Camille Henderson approached the back of the tall cowboy.

She'd only been on the ranch a few weeks, but she'd fallen in love with all the Randalls. Their unique take on life made sharing a house with them a lot of fun. She waited for Jake to turn around, expecting a big grin on his face.

When the man slowly turned to face her, she gasped in surprise. "You're—you're not Jake!"

"No, I'm not." He didn't smile, but that was one of only a few differences between him and Jake Randall, head of the Randall clan.

Both men were tall, broad shouldered, narrow hipped. The hair was the same color, dark, almost black, but this man's was trimmed a little shorter, more stylishly cut. Their eyes were the same chocolate brown, only this man's eyes didn't smile.

"Who are you?"

He stared at her, giving no response, and a shiver rushed through her. She took a step backward.

"Jake, did Camille tell you—?"

Camille spun around, relieved to hear B.J. approaching. "It's not Jake."

"I can see," B. J. Randall agreed, her eyes curious. She stepped toward the man, her hand extended. "Hello, I'm B.J., Jake's wife. I'm sorry we mistook you for my husband, but you're remarkably similar."

Though he took B.J.'s hand, Camille read reluctance in his action. No one could resist B.J.; however, this man continued to keep his silence.

"May we help you? Are you lost?" B.J. finally asked.

Camille held her breath. Surely this man's resemblance to Jake couldn't be a coincidence.

"I need to speak to whoever is head of the family." His voice was husky, as if emotion flooded him, but he held himself stiffly erect, staring, no hint of a smile on his face.

B.J. exchanged a look of concern with Camille, then faced the man again. "That would be my husband, Jake Randall. He's due home any moment. I thought he'd already arrived in a new Lexus when you pulled up. That's why we greeted you so strangely. If you'll come in, we'll—" She stopped her long-winded explanation at the sound of another approaching vehicle.

Camille turned around to verify that it was Jake's pickup coming home. She returned her gaze to the stranger's face, anxious to see his reaction when he saw Jake. Their resemblance was eerie.

Jake pulled his truck past them, close to the house, parked and got out. He made a beeline for B.J., all his attention focused on his wife.

That was one of the nice things about the Randall men. They were one-woman men, dedicated to their wives. Camille liked that, especially after her experience.

Jake slid his left arm around B.J., and looked at the other man in surprise. "Hello. I'm Jake Randall. I don't believe we've met."

Camille held her breath as the stranger stared first at Jake, then at the extended hand. Surely he was going to shake Jake's hand. It would be an insult—

Finally, the man moved, taking Jake's hand in his. But he said nothing.

"Your name?" Jake asked, his voice changing from warm geniality to tension.

"Griff—"

"Aieoooooow!" A male howl of pain rose in the air, followed by staccato thumps and a fierce neigh from a disturbed horse.

All four of them turned in the direction of the noise, coming from one of the barns.

"Damn!" Jake muttered. As he began to run, he called over his shoulder, "Someone find Pete. That sounds like the new bronc he brought home yesterday!"

"Camille," B.J. pleaded as she followed Jake.

Camille exchanged startled looks with the stranger. Pete had come in early today because he and Janie, his wife, had taken the twins in for their checkup, but she thought they'd come back an hour ago. She started running to the house.

Halfway to the porch, she saw Toby, B.J.'s eight-year-old son, come out the back door. "Toby? Is Uncle Pete in the house?"

"Yeah."

"Tell him to come to the barn, quick!" she exclaimed, and reversed her direction. She wanted to see what was happening. She noted, as she ran, that the stranger was no longer in sight, but his car was still there.

Charging into the barn, she discovered Jake and the stranger in a large box stall, with B.J. standing outside it. Jake was starting to lift an unconscious man from the hay while the stranger held the head of the horse.

Camille stared as the man appeared to be talking to the animal, caressing its head and neck. Then she noted several boards almost pushed apart from the frame of the stall.

B.J. moved to help Jake, but he stopped her. "Stay outside. I don't want you in here in case Griff can't keep the animal under control."

B.J. did as he said, but she kept anxious eyes on her husband and his burden.

"Can I help?" Camille asked softly.

"Get some blankets from the tack room," B.J. said just as quietly.

Camille slipped past B.J. and hurried to do as she asked. She'd already learned in the two weeks she'd been on the ranch not to startle the horses. She took extra care with this one. He'd almost kicked down the wall.

Pete erupted into the quiet of the barn, Toby on his heels, just as Jake got the unconscious man past the gate of the stall. B.J. took the blankets from Camille and began making a pallet on the floor.

The noise from the latest arrivals sent spasms of fear through the horse, and the stranger redoubled his efforts to calm him.

"What's going on?" Pete demanded, then immediately lowered his voice. "What's he doing in there with that horse? The thing's wild."

"Too bad you didn't tell your new hand," Jake muttered, taking a deep breath as he stood from putting the man on the pallet.

"Barney? Is he hurt bad?" Pete asked, kneeling down beside the man.

"He hasn't come to," B.J. said. "Is Anna home?" Anna, Brett Randall's wife, was a nurse who delivered babies in the area.

"She's giving that birthing class at Doc's office, remember?" Camille said. Her gaze kept darting to the dark stranger.

"We're going to need the ambulance," B.J., the local veterinarian, determined.

"Toby, go get my cell phone out of the truck," Jake ordered, and the boy scooted out of the barn at once.

Pete seemed concerned about his employee, Barney, but, like Camille, his gaze kept drifting back to the stranger, who remained with the horse.

When Toby returned, Jake made the emergency call. B.J. remained beside the injured man, but Pete moved to the stall.

"Maybe you should come out now, before he gets difficult again," he suggested, but his words sounded like an order.

The man patted the horse one last time and turned toward the gate. To everyone's surprise, the animal docilely followed him.

"Watch out!" Pete called hoarsely.

The man ignored his warning, reached the gate, opened it, then closed it behind him. Then he patted the horse again.

"Who are you?" Pete demanded, his brows furrowed.

The man gave him a steady regard, but he didn't answer.

"Name's Griff," Jake said. "Right?"

The man nodded.

Pete continued to stare. "Well, you shouldn't— Hell, Jake, the man looks just like you!" Pete exclaimed.

A groan from the man on the floor caught everyone's attention. Pete squatted down beside him. "Easy, Barney. We've got help on the way."

"Sorry, Pete," the older man muttered. "Wanted to show you I could—" He stopped, grimacing as he drew breath.

"What was your role in this fiasco?" Pete asked

the stranger. Camille held her breath, anxious for an explanation of the man's arrival.

But it was Jake who answered. "He was introducing himself to me when we heard Barney howl and your new acquisition protesting whatever was going on."

"I told Barney we were going to give Rambo here his shots this afternoon, but we were waiting for B.J. I guess he decided to go ahead by himself." Pete frowned down at the man, who had his eyes closed.

In the distance, Camille heard a siren. "I think the ambulance is getting close."

"Toby, you want to go outside and show them where they're needed?" Jake suggested.

"Aw, Daddy, I want to stay here and—"

Jake shot his stepson a stern look, and the little boy broke off his protest. With dragging boots, he shuffled out of the barn to do his father's bidding.

Camille smiled. Jake and Toby were a pair. It was hard to believe he wasn't Toby's biological father. B.J. had been widowed when Toby was a baby. Jake and Toby shared the same coloring, and now, after B.J. and Toby moved here a couple of years ago, Toby patterned his behavior after his new dad.

Camille's gaze came back to the stranger, who was carefully studying all of them, but most especially the two Randall men. He had the same dark hair and brown eyes as the Randalls. But he couldn't have intentionally developed their expressions, their mannerisms, because he'd never seen them before.

So why was he just like them?

The ambulance, from Rawhide, had arrived and Toby led the two paramedics into the barn. Everyone stood back while they examined the man and rolled out a stretcher.

"Looks like busted ribs and a mild concussion," one of the medics said to B.J. "We'd better get him into town for Doc to look at him." They laid Barney on the stretcher and rolled him out to the ambulance, with everyone trailing.

Once they closed the back door of the ambulance, Pete said to the driver, "Tell Doc to fix him up. I'll be in after dinner to check on him, unless it's more serious than you think."

"Naw, Pete, he'll be all right. I'll pass the message on to Doc."

Silence fell over the group as they watched the ambulance drive away. Then Jake turned to the new arrival. "Griff, I owe you thanks. I might be in the same shape as Barney if you hadn't grabbed that mangy horse."

"No problem."

"How did you settle him down?" Pete asked.

The man shrugged his shoulders. "I just talked to him."

Pete studied the man. Camille wondered if Pete realized how expensively dressed the man was. In Wyoming, everyone dressed in jeans and a shirt. The man was wearing jeans, but with a designer label. And his starched shirt didn't look as if it came cheap, either. She knew the Rolex on his wrist cost a bundle.

"You lookin' for work?" Pete asked finally.

"No."

As if he hadn't heard the abrupt answer, Pete continued, "'Cause I could use a good hand. I run rodeo stock. Sometimes they're hard to deal with."

"Sorry."

Not a talkative man, Camille decided with a grin.

"Whether you want a job or not," Jake said, "you earned a good meal. Come on in. Dinner will be ready in a few minutes."

"No. I don't want to intrude. I need to have a word with you, that's all," the man said, his gaze meeting Jake's.

"With me?"

"Yeah, you're head of the family, aren't you?" He shifted his gaze from Jake to B.J. and back again. "That's what your wife said."

Jake's lips twitched as he looked first at B.J. and then Pete. "Hell, yes, I'm the head of the family. But I don't think I can talk until after I feed myself. Come on, Griff. We won't poison you."

Taking B.J.'s hand, he led the way into the house, expecting everyone to follow. Everyone did, except the stranger. Camille watched out of the corner of her eye as the man clearly stood debating the invitation.

She unconsciously gave a sigh of relief as he finally began walking after them. Startled, she questioned her interest in the man's capitulation. After all, it meant nothing to her. She wasn't part of the Randall clan. Well, except by connection.

Her father had briefly been married to Megan's mother. They'd divorced, but she and Megan had remained friends. Since Megan had married Chad, that made Camille an ex-step-sister to one of the Randall wives.

All of which had nothing to do with the intense interest she felt in the man behind her. When his arm came around her to hold the back door open, her breath caught in her throat. He was as big as the other Randalls—but he wasn't one, of course, or they would've recognized him.

Besides, they had no other family members—

Suddenly, she gasped and whirled around to stare at the man behind her.

"What's wrong?" he asked, his voice gravelly.

"Nothing!" she snapped, and faced forward again, passing through the mudroom to the kitchen, hoping the heat in her cheeks would quickly dissipate. But the thought that had popped into her head left her mind spinning.

She'd read about such events in books. Was she going to see it played out before her? And would it hurt Jake and the others? Because it suddenly occurred to her that this man could be an illegitimate brother.

Which would mean their father, Gus Randall, had betrayed their mother.

Oh, dear.

"What's going on out there?" Red, their cowboy housekeeper, called as they all entered the kitchen. "We heard the ambulance."

"Barney tried to work with the new bronc I brought in. He got pounded," Pete explained.

"He gonna be all right?" Red asked calmly. He'd seen many a disaster in his long years on the ranch.

"Yeah. Concussion and ribs," Pete added.

"Red, we need to set an extra plate for dinner," Jake said, changing the subject. "Griff, here, helped me out, and I invited him to eat with us."

"Please, if it's any trouble—" the man began.

"No trouble at all," Red said. Then he looked at Jake. "Did you warn him?"

Jake shook his head, and everyone grinned. Camille saw the puzzled look on the man's handsome face. She'd had the same reaction. Since she was closest to him, she said softly, "It's rather a large family. With a lot of babies."

B.J. sighed. "I'm afraid Camille is right. But we feed the babies first and put them in the playpens," she said, gesturing to the three playpens that lined the far wall.

"Not me!" Toby protested. "I'm too old for those things," he assured the man, stretching to look taller.

"And you're big enough to lend a hand, pardner," Red added. "Start hauling these platters to the table."

"I'll help, too, Red," Camille said as she moved to the stove. Unfortunately, she didn't allow enough space as she cut through the men and bumped into the newcomer's rock-hard chest. His large, warm hands caught her shoulders as she bounced back from him. "Sorry," she muttered, trying to hide her reaction to his touch. The shivers coursing through her body didn't make sense.

"No problem," he returned.

"Where's Mildred?" Jake asked, naming Red's wife, his assistant and B.J.'s aunt all rolled into one lady.

"She's up helping Janie with all the little ones. With Anna teaching that class and B.J. working and Megan gone to town, she needed help."

"I'll go hurry them up," B.J. said as she headed for the stairs.

"I'll show Griff where he can wash up," Jake said.

As the man followed Jake, Red stopped him. "Hell, you look just like the others. Who are you, boy?"

The man seemed startled by Red's frankness. Pete rescued him. "He's a hell of a horseman, and I'm trying to hire him."

"Don't mind Red," Jake added. "He's not known for his subtlety."

Red snorted as the three men left the room. "No need to circle the mountain for days before climbing it. You see the resemblance?" he asked Camille.

"Yes, but Red, what if he's an illegitimate son? What if their daddy—?"

"Nope. Their daddy didn't mess around. Even after their mother died when Chad was born, he didn't have any women."

She sighed. "Then I don't understand it. I mean,

everyone is supposed to have a double in the world, but I've never seen—''

''What have you never seen?'' Chad asked, a grin on his face as he and Brett, the two youngest of the Randall brothers, strolled into the kitchen.

Brett ignored his brother's question. ''Is Anna back yet?''

''Or Megan?'' Chad added.

The Randall men liked to keep track of their women. It restored Camille's faith in love.

''Nope. Neither of 'em. And dinner's almost ready.''

Camille carried another platter to the table, this one full of chicken-fried steak. Toby was putting out napkins. Then he began pulling high chairs to the table. They needed three high chairs, for Elizabeth, two and a half years old, Chad and Megan's child; for Caroline, nineteen months, Toby's little sister; and one for Victoria, Brett and Anna's baby, the youngest at seven months.

The three-year-old twins, Richard and Russell, Pete and Janie's boys, used booster seats.

When Camille had first arrived, it had taken her a few days to recover from the shock of them all. But the longer she stayed, the more she fell in love with a family who worked together, pitching in whenever one of the adults needed an extra hand.

It sounded like a thundering herd coming down the stairs as Mildred, B.J. and Janie arrived with all the children.

Mass pandemonium reigned for a few moments

as they all tried to get the children settled in their places and start dinner. Even Toby played a role, helping the twins. He always said the menfolk should stick together. But he was sweetly tender with the girls.

Jake and Griff returned to the kitchen in the middle of all the settling in, and Camille grinned as she saw the startled expression on Griff's face. It was an improvement over the grim look he'd shown them earlier.

She wondered what he'd look like if he smiled. He caught her staring, and she hurried back to the sink to find something to do to hide her red cheeks.

"It'll be our turn in a minute," Jake assured him. "Our kids don't mess around when it comes to dinner."

"How true," B.J. agreed with a big smile. "They take after their fathers."

"And that's how we like it, sweetheart." Jake stroked a strand of hair behind her ear that had escaped from B.J.'s long braid. "Need any help?"

"No, I think we've got it covered. Do I hear a car?"

Brett and Chad met each other at the window. "Two cars. Megan and Anna are home," Chad announced. Both of them headed to the door, eager to greet their wives.

By the time both couples had returned to the kitchen, the children were fed. Everyone grabbed a child to transfer him or her to a playpen, though the twins protested, asking to stay with Toby.

In no time, Mildred and Red had cleaned up and invited everyone to sit down at the huge table.

Jake led Griff to the last place on the side next to his seat, at the head of the table. Camille found herself next to him. She shivered again as his broad shoulder brushed against hers.

What was wrong with her? She'd been around men before. She'd even been engaged recently. Before disaster had struck her. So why did this man affect her so? She eased along the bench, trying to put some distance between them, but Brett, on her other side, wasn't shifting.

Jake offered an introduction of Griff to the newly arrived family members. After the blessing was asked and the plates began making their way around the table, Brett noted what had struck the others.

"Man, you sure look like the rest of us, Jake in particular," Brett said. "Are you some long-lost relative?"

Griff, who had been serving himself from the steak platter, stilled. Then he carefully put the meat on his plate and laid down his utensils.

His chin came up and his lips firmed into a straight line. "Yes. I probably should've introduced myself before I sat down. If you want me to leave—"

Camille watched him, fascinated and unexpectedly anxious, but she also caught a glimpse of Jake out of the corner of her eye. He didn't seem alarmed at the man's words. Just curious.

"We're not going to take back our invitation,

Griff," Jake said quietly. "You more than earned a meal when you helped out in the barn. But why don't you tell us just who you are."

He cleared his throat and stiffened his shoulders, as if he was about to impart bad news. "I'm Margaret's son. Griffin Randall."

Chapter Two

In the silence that fell, Chad stared at Griff and asked, "Who the hell—uh, heck," he repaired after Megan elbowed him in the ribs, "is Margaret?"

Red didn't wait for an answer. Seated at the other end of the table, he stood, his face paling, and began walking toward Griff.

Ah, here it came, Griff thought almost with relief. He'd been a little lost in the midst of the warm hospitality of these people. He'd expected anger.

He stood to meet what was coming head-on.

"You're Margaret's son?" Red asked softly, with wonder in his eyes. "How is she? Where is she?"

"Who is she?" Chad repeated, frowning.

"She's Dad's sister," Jake explained quietly.

Red came closer, and Griff thought the old man intended to punch him out. Then, all at once, Red enveloped him in a bear hug. Griff reared back in surprise.

"Sorry, boy, I startled you, didn't I?"

Griff frowned at the older man and nodded his head. "You're not angry?"

"Why would I be? We worried about Margaret for years. Gus finally gave her up for dead."

"She is dead," Griffin said harshly. He watched the various reactions of the people gathered around the table.

Jake stood and extended his hand. Again Griff stared at the gesture. Finally, he gripped Jake's strong hand and looked into his unknown cousin's gaze.

"Welcome home, Griff."

"This is not my home." His words were uttered with the anger he'd expected from them.

"Maybe not, but it should've been," Jake said, sitting back down. "Don't let your food get cold. We'll find out why you're here later."

Griff stared at Jake and then Red. The older man patted his arm and returned to his seat at the head of the table.

These people weren't what he expected. In looks, yes, though it had startled him to see how much he resembled his cousins. But, somehow, after listening to his mother's heartbreaking words when she talked of her home, he'd expected a lot of hostility.

And he felt a lot of hostility inside himself. His mother had suffered because of these people.

Or their relatives.

With a sigh, he sat back down. The lady beside him, Camille, he thought her name was, silently offered a plate of biscuits. When he glared at her, she gave him a sympathetic smile.

A smile that made her soft blond hair, her blue

eyes, her patrician features, even more enticing. And when those attractions were attached to a slender body with curves in all the right places, something he'd noted earlier, she could've been a movie star. Why didn't she belong to one of the testosterone-filled men around the table?

Because they already had their own beauties.

So where did she come from?

"When did your mother die?" Red asked, drawing Griff's attention back to the present.

"Last week."

His terse response drew a gasp from Red.

With eyes staring into the distance, Red muttered, "All this time…"

Mildred reached out for her husband's hand. He turned to her, a grateful smile on his face. "She was my first love, you know, sweetheart. We grew up together. But she had no time for me."

Griff felt relief fill him. For a moment, he'd wondered if Red was his father. His greatest anger was directed toward that unknown man who'd taken his pleasure from Griff's mother and then refused to be responsible for the result.

Brett seemed unaware of Griff's reaction. His attention was on Red. "Is she the reason you didn't mess with the ladies till Mildred came along?" He grinned. "I didn't know you were hiding a broken heart all those years."

"There's lots you don't know, boy," Red growled.

Jake uttered one quiet word, and it underlined his position in the family. "Brett."

Though Brett continued to grin, he stopped teasing Red.

Griff studied Red, trying to picture his mother as she'd been when Red knew her. She would've been better off with Red, who seemed a decent man, than with the one who'd betrayed her.

"Would you like more tea?" Camille asked, leaning toward him.

He drew in her scent, finding it disturbing. "No, thank you."

His gaze followed her as she crossed the kitchen, unable to resist watching her.

Jake leaned toward him. "Camille is Megan's step-sister. She's not a Randall."

Griff blinked several times, his gaze returning to the man beside him. When he realized Jake had noted his interest in Camille, he hastily backpedaled. "I'm not— I'll be leaving as soon as possible."

"Leaving for where?" Pete asked, the first time he'd spoken since Griff's revelation.

"Chicago."

"Is that where Margaret lived?" Red asked.

"Yes."

Another silence filled the room, the only noise the scrape of silverware against the dishes.

"How the hell did you learn how to handle horses in Chicago?" Pete finally demanded, staring at him.

Griff didn't answer at once. Then he looked Pete in the eye. "My mother taught me. She insisted I grow up around horses. We frequented a riding stable on the outskirts of town.''

''But you know more than how to ride. You calmed Rambo without any problem.''

''Margaret,'' Red said succinctly.

''What?'' Pete asked, his gaze turning to the older man.

''Margaret was a dab hand with the horses. Better'n Gus.'' Red rubbed his face, as if remembering was painful. ''She could talk to them.''

Griff nodded.

''Well, the job's still there, if you want it,'' Pete said.

''Hell, Pete, he probably owns half the ranch,'' Chad interjected, heat in his words.

For the first time, Griff heard the anger he'd expected. He didn't want their ranch. But he wasn't going to relieve them of that fear just yet. And fear was visible on several faces around the table.

But not on Jake's.

''We'll talk after dinner,'' he reiterated. ''Pass the potatoes, Chad.''

WHEN JAKE LED the way into an office near the kitchen, Griff followed without protest. It was time to clear everything up. The other three Randall brothers gathered around the desk as Jake sat down behind it, leaving a chair for Griffin.

Again Griffin noted Jake's authority. None of the others spoke, waiting for their oldest brother to take the lead.

"Why don't you tell us why you're here, Griff?" he said calmly.

Griff sat up straighter. "My mother fought cancer the past year. Her dying request was to be buried on the ranch. I promised her."

Jake nodded but said nothing.

They all sat in silence. Finally, Chad spoke. "That's all you want?"

"Yes."

Several of the men released pent-up breaths, but Griff didn't bother to check to see who it was. "You don't have a problem with my burying my mother here?" he asked Jake, wanting to be sure he'd understood the nod.

"Of course not. My father would have been pleased. He would've been more pleased to have Margaret come home before her death. He made some effort to find her but was unsuccessful."

Griffin nodded, acknowledging what Jake said, relieved that his mother hadn't been totally forgotten. Maybe her bitterness shouldn't have been so complete.

"How do you know all this?" Chad asked. "I'd never heard of her before."

Jake shrugged. "Dad talked about her sometimes when we were boys. And Red has said some things." He shook his head. "Dad's income was dependent on Granddad, and the old man didn't want to look for Margaret. He was mad at her."

Griff didn't ask any questions. His mother had talked about her past frequently.

"Why?" Pete asked. "Why was Granddad mad at her?"

Jake shrugged, as if he didn't know, but Griff wasn't sure whether to believe he knew nothing or simply wanted to save Griff's face.

"My mother was having an affair," Griff said softly. "Her father found out about it and jumped her pretty hard. She was supposed to stop…and she didn't. When she realized she was pregnant, she ran. The old man had promised to throw her out anyway."

"That's pretty hard," Brett muttered, frowning.

"Yeah. She was seventeen, pregnant and on her own."

Griff tried to keep the bitterness from his voice, but he knew he wasn't successful.

"Hey, maybe Red is your—" Chad broke off, apology on his face.

"No. Her lover was married." Griff ducked his head, then faced the others. "I know it's no excuse, but she was young, headstrong."

"Hell, man, we're not going to sit in judgment on your mother," Jake assured him. "Do you know your father's name?"

"No. She never told me." He stared at the bookshelves that lined one wall of the room. "She said he didn't want her or their baby."

It always amazed Griff that he could feel any pain about that rejection. The man wasn't someone he would want for a father, a man who'd break his marriage vows and then deny responsibility. Not the kind of father any man would choose. But it still hurt. As it had hurt his mother her entire life.

"Are you planning to find out who he is?" Brett asked. "Is that part of why you came back?"

"No. Just to bury my mother."

"We'll start making arrangements tomorrow," Jake assured him. "In the meantime, we want you to stay here with us."

"No. I'll find a room in Rawhide," Griffin said. He'd driven through the small town on his way from the airport in Casper.

Pete chuckled. "You'd better take Jake up on his offer, Griff. That fleabag motel in Rawhide isn't worth the bucks you'd have to pay."

"Maybe not, but that doesn't matter. And you seem to have a full house here," Griff argued.

"Yeah, we do," Jake agreed with a big grin. "I planned it that way. You'll find it hard to believe, but four years ago, there weren't any women or children on the ranch."

Griff saw the pleasure on his cousin's face. Then Griff frowned. "But Toby has to be seven or eight."

"Yeah. He's my step-son." Pride filled Jake's voice.

Griff decided Toby was a lucky little boy.

"Well, the four of you have certainly made up for short time." He smiled as he stood and stuck out his hand to Jake. "Thank you for letting me keep my promise. I'll call you tomorrow to—"

"Man, you're not going anywhere," Jake said even as he grasped Griff's hand. "Red's room is behind the kitchen, with its own bath. Since he married Mildred, they live in B.J.'s old house just past the second barn. You'll be comfortable in his old room, and it'll keep you out of the major traffic patterns in the house.''

Griff didn't see any disagreement on any of the men's faces. Curiosity and wariness filled him. He'd lived all his life alone, except for his mother. He'd had no other family. Suddenly, he had enough family to fill a big house. And they wanted him to stay.

Jake led the way from the room as if he assumed Griff had agreed, just as he had led the way to dinner.

Chad grinned at him. "Jake always gets his way."

"I can see that. I'm not putting anyone out?"

"Naw," Brett assured him. "We're always having guests. Camille's been here a couple of weeks already."

Griff frowned. That young lady was a good reason for him not to stay at the Randalls'.

"Pretty, isn't she?" Chad added. "Good thing she isn't a Randall."

"Why?" Griff snapped.

"'Cause it wouldn't be right for you to look at your cousin the way you look at Camille," Chad said, and walked out.

Griff wanted to protest, to say he hadn't noticed Camille, but that would be a blatant lie.

Brett grinned and followed his brother.

Pete gestured for Griff to precede him. As he did

so, Pete said softly, "Don't worry. We've all been there. That's why we have a houseful of babies."

"I have no intention of—" Griff began.

"Nope. We didn't, either," Pete assured him, his grin as big as his brothers'.

CAMILLE STOOD under the trees, wrapped in a jacket and watching as they lowered the casket into the ground. Only a few words had been spoken, first by the Randalls' minister, then by Griffin Randall.

Camille decided he was a private man. Though obviously moved by his mother's death, he kept his remarks brief and impersonal. Just as he had since his arrival several days ago. She couldn't keep from being aware of his presence, but it wasn't because he called attention to himself.

As they turned away from the small plot where all the Randalls had been buried, Camille wondered what would happen now. She'd watched Griffin from a distance as his cousins showed him the ranch. He'd seemed at ease among them, though never laughing, or hardly even smiling.

While he'd talked with the Randall brothers, he'd avoided the women. Particularly her. Camille shook her head. It was silly to take his behavior personally. After all, his interest would be in his blood kin, known to him for the first time.

And when he chose any of the Randall wives over her for assistance, conversation or friendship, it was probably because they were connected to him by marriage.

Besides, she wasn't interested in men right now. Maybe sometime in the future, though she wasn't sure. Her fiancé's betrayal had made her cautious.

The Randalls had been the perfect antidote for her bitterness and cynicism, in addition to giving her time to decide her future. But she wasn't ready to risk her heart again. Not yet.

"What happens now?" she whispered to Megan.

"The people who came knew Margaret. Jake will invite them back to the house so they can talk to Griffin. I hope he's prepared for that." Megan studied the silent man standing among his cousins. "I feel so sorry for him."

"Will he lay claim to any of the ranch?" Camille asked. The topic hadn't been mentioned since Chad had brought it up that first night.

"Jake told Chad that Griff didn't legally have any right to the ranch, because their grandfather left it all to Gus, Margaret's brother. But Jake has talked to the others, and they all feel Griffin should receive something."

"That would be fair, but wouldn't it be awful to break up the ranch?" Camille had been impressed with the joint ownership the Randalls had.

"They'll work out something. Come on, Chad is waving to us." The two women hurried to the car they'd ridden in.

Back at the house, the number of people seemed more than it had been graveside. Probably because they were now enclosed. Red and Mildred had prepared a buffet for the guests, spread out on the long table.

Jake stayed by Griffin's side, introducing neighbors as they approached. Most of them were Red's age or older, though several were accompanied by younger people.

"Hello, dear, I don't believe I've met you," an elderly lady said, leaning toward Camille.

"I'm Camille Henderson, Megan's step-sister."

"Henderson? I didn't remember that was Megan's name. Would you two be kin to the Hendersons near Buffalo?"

Camille exchanged a grin with Megan but didn't bother explaining the difference in her and Megan's last names. "No, I'm afraid not. I'm from Colorado."

"Oh. I don't know any Hendersons in Colorado." The woman's gaze lit on Griffin.

"That boy sure is a Randall, isn't he? Strange he would have the same last name, though. Didn't he take his father's name?"

Camille had no idea what to say. Fortunately, Megan spoke. "His mother never married."

The old woman gasped, as if Megan had revealed a shocking fact. "You mean he's illegitimate?"

Chad, having approached unnoticed, slid his arm around Megan and stared at their guest. "He's a Randall, Mrs. Widdaker. That's all we need to know."

"I know, my boy, but still— Well, I suppose those wicked cities make it hard for a young woman.

She should've stayed here. She wouldn't have gotten into such trouble, if she had.''

Much to Camille's surprise, Griffin stepped forward to speak to Chad and overheard the woman's words.

"You're wrong. My mother got pregnant while she lived here. In Chicago, she managed to find acceptance and make a living. Something she couldn't have done here.''

The woman's shocked face created a tense moment. Then she apologized and hurried away.

"Damn, Griff, I don't think you should've told Mrs. Widdaker that little fact," Chad protested. "She's the worst gossip in the entire county.''

"It doesn't matter. Unless it embarrasses you. You've all been most gracious, and I wouldn't want to cause you any shame.''

Jake wandered up. "What's wrong?''

Camille kept silent.

"What makes you think something's wrong?'' Griff said stiffly.

"'Cause you're looking like you did when you first arrived, as if you're waiting for an attack. Did someone say something wrong?''

"Yeah, him," Chad said laconically.

"Chad, that's not fair," Camille hastily said, before she realized Griffin wouldn't appreciate any defense.

"Well, it sure wasn't me.''

Jake ignored Chad and looked at Griffin. "What happened?''

Griffin shrugged. "I mentioned that Mother was pregnant with me before she left town."

"To Mrs. Widdaker," Chad added.

Jake groaned. "Well, you certainly know how to stir the pot."

"What difference does it make? I'm leaving tomorrow. I'll apologize if it brings any embarrassment to you, but that could be the only reason it would matter."

"I've been meaning to talk to you about your plans," Jake said. "After everyone goes home, we'll have a chat."

Camille thought it was a measure of the friendship that had developed between the cousins that Griff only nodded, showing no stress about Jake's request.

She wondered what Jake had in mind.

Even though she wasn't staying permanently at the ranch, she hoped Jake intended to invite Griff to stay. The loneliness that surrounded him ate into her peace.

She almost laughed aloud as she recognized how silly her thoughts were. She was no better off than Griff as far as family. In fact, her situation was lonelier. All she had was Megan, and she wasn't blood kin.

Griffin had four cousins and their wives and children. And somewhere, he probably had a father.

"Mr. Randall," Mrs. Widdaker called from across the room, pushing her way toward them. "I know who your father is!"

Chapter Three

Everyone in the large room stopped talking and stared first at Mrs. Widdaker and then at Griffin. He clenched his teeth, fighting the urge to inform the entire county what he thought about his father.

Then he started as soft, warm fingers slid around one of his clenched fists. The one closest to Camille. He stared first at her hand and then at the beautiful woman beside him. Did she think he needed protection?

"It must be Red," Mrs. Widdaker announced, delighted to be the center of attention.

Before Griff could say anything, Red stepped forward. "It damn well isn't. Not that I wouldn't like to claim Griff as my son. But I'm not his father. Margaret and I were friends, that's all."

Jake laid a warm hand on Griffin's shoulder, as if hoping to silence an angry response, but Griff spoke anyway. "I wish you were, Red. But since we both know you're not, we'll drop the subject. I don't have any interest in the man, whoever he is."

"But—" Mrs. Widdaker began, only to be cut off by B.J., the Randall closest to her.

"Have you tasted my aunt Mildred's broccoli-cheese dip, Mrs. Widdaker? She's going to enter it in the state fair in Douglas next year."

To Griff's surprise, the woman was distracted by B.J.'s words. He frowned.

Jake whispered as he offered a pat on Griff's shoulder before taking his hand away, "Mrs. Widdaker always takes home the blue ribbon. She wouldn't take any competition lightly."

Griff nodded, but he was distracted by those warm fingers that continued to hold on to him. Finally, he tugged on his hand, and Camille jumped, as if she'd forgotten what she held. He leaned over. "Did you think I needed protection?"

Her cheeks bloomed with color, only increasing her beauty, but she didn't look at him. "I—I was concerned."

Because the comfort she offered was unusual, charming, tempting, he spoke more coolly than he should have. "I'm a big boy. I can take care of myself."

"Of course. Excuse me." If he'd been cool, Camille's tone was frigid. Before he could offer an apology, she moved away.

He looked guiltily at Jake.

"You say something wrong?" he asked.

"She— I—I guess so."

"So you apologize later. She'll forgive you."

"It might be best if I don't, Jake. I may have

given all of you the wrong idea. I have no interest in—in a relationship. I don't want anyone to get the wrong idea.''

Jake raised an eyebrow. "You sound like some of my brothers when I urged them to marry.''

Griff couldn't help smiling at the speculative look in Jake's eye. "Don't even think it, cousin. I'd be a whole lot tougher sell than those guys.''

"Why do you think that?''

"Because romantic love wasn't a happy topic at our house. My mother never forgave the man who betrayed her. She never found comfort with another man. I grew up hearing the catechism of pain and heartbreak.''

"Look around you, Griff. I'm sorry for your mother, but others find true happiness.'' Jake focused his gaze on his wife, holding Caroline as she chatted with the neighbors. "Some of us get so lucky we're afraid to breathe.''

"My point exactly. I don't have any trouble breathing, because I'm in control of my happiness.'' Griff caught his gaze drifting to a certain blonde, but he jerked his gaze away before anyone could notice. He hoped.

"Uh-huh,'' Jake agreed, but there was laughter in his voice. "We'll see.''

"Besides, I'm leaving in the morning.''

"Why?''

Jake's question startled Griff, the second time he'd been shaken from his thoughts this afternoon. "Because I've done what I came to do.''

CAMILLE COULDN'T BELIEVE she'd embarrassed herself as she had. She had no connection to Griffin Randall, and he'd made it clear he had no interest in her.

But her heart ached for him.

She wasn't in love with him. No, that was a game she wasn't anxious to play again so soon. But he was hurting. Like the puppy she'd brought home one day. Or the friend whose family life was awful. Or the children she'd tried to help through one of the charities she sponsored.

She'd suffered through her father's death six months ago. She knew how much it hurt to lose both parents.

She'd only been trying to help Griffin, but he thought she was coming on to him. Well, he could suffer on his own now. She wasn't getting near him again.

"What happened?" B.J. asked, stopping beside Camille. "Did he take Jake's offer?"

"What? Who?" Camille asked.

"Griff. Did Jake make his offer?"

"Not while I was around. Nothing happened."

B.J. studied her. "Did he say something to upset you?"

"No. I'm fine. Shall we clear the food? People are starting to leave."

"No. We'll all gather around the table and have supper in a little while. I doubt if many of us got much to eat."

"B.J.?" Jake called from across the room, motioning for her to join him.

"Want me to take Caroline?" Camille immediately offered. "Is she ready for her nap?"

"Oh, bless you, Camille. Yes, she is. Would you mind taking her upstairs?"

In answer, Camille reached out for the little girl. She'd been willing to help with the kids ever since she arrived. After all, it was a novelty for her. But she was even more eager today because she wanted to be far away from the cold man across the room.

As THEY GATHERED around the table when the last of the guests had gone, Griff saw that Camille wasn't there. He kept waiting for someone else to notice, but with all the noise of the family, no one did.

Finally, he leaned over to Jake. "Isn't Camille going to eat?"

Jake then noticed the empty chair beside Griffin. He looked to his right at B.J. "Where is Camille?"

B.J. also seemed surprised. "I don't know. She put Caroline down for her nap." She leaned forward. "Anyone seen Camille?"

"I'll go check on her," Megan offered. Before she left the room, she stared at her husband. "You keep an eye on Elizabeth."

"Always, sweetheart," he agreed with a big grin.

Griff turned away, unwilling to admire the love that flowed between the couples in the room. He had no intention of being persuaded to believe in happily-ever-after.

Megan entered the room with Camille right behind her. Griff turned his stare to his plate. It was the only safe spot in the room.

Camille came to an abrupt halt at the other end of the table. "Um, do you think you could all shift down one seat? I have something I need to discuss with Mildred."

Griff whipped his head up and stared at the young woman. Her normal seat was beside him. Did she have to make her antagonism so blatant? It irritated him that she was announcing her displeasure so openly.

None of the Randalls questioned her, however, good-naturedly shifting down the table. Which put Brett next to Griffin.

"Stepped in it, did you?"

Griff glared at the young man beside him. "Not at all. You heard her. She wants to talk to Mildred."

Brett laughed. "Sure."

Griff returned his attention to his plate.

As a contented silence fell over the group, Jake put down his fork. "So, Griff, we've been talking."

Griff frowned. Jake's words seemed to have some significance. He waited, his attention on the man beside him.

"You don't legally have any claim to our ranch."

Griffin straightened in his chair and opened his mouth, but Jake held up a hand, stopping him.

"Let me finish," Jake asked. When Griffin subsided, he said, "We think you should share in the Randall legacy, however. Dad would've wanted that."

"Jake, you don't owe me anything," Griff hurriedly said. In fact, he didn't want their offer, whatever it might be. He didn't want to owe anyone. Ever.

"We're not offering to carve up the land for you," Jake assured him with a grin. "But we do have something in mind."

"Jake, really—"

"We want to buy the ranch next to ours. You could still live here with us. We'll show you how to do everything, share our ranch hands with you. With your skills with the horses, you could—"

"Jake, I can't accept." Griffin tried to keep a smile on his face, but he felt it disappearing.

Jake wouldn't stop. "You don't understand, Griff. We may not have Persian rugs and priceless art, but we have oil wells. We have more money than we need. We were thinking about buying old man Haney's place anyway, but we'd have to hire more men. It's a perfect solution."

Griffin closed his eyes, unable to look at the happy expectation in Jake's eyes, even in his brothers'. He'd never met such selfless, good men. "No!"

Chad finally broke the silence that followed Griffin's response. "The land's not good enough for you?"

Griffin drew a deep breath, but he kept his gaze fixed on his plate. He couldn't face these people.

"I have to return to Chicago."

Brett spoke up. "You have a woman waiting for you?"

Someone down the table gasped. Griffin was tempted to lean forward, to see if it was Camille who reacted so noisily. But he didn't dare.

"No."

"Then what's in Chicago?" Chad demanded.

"My life!" Griffin retorted.

When silence again greeted his words, he sighed. "Look, I appreciate your hospitality. You've been generous, kind—hell, you've been damn saintly!" he exclaimed. "But I don't belong here."

"You know," Jake said calmly, after taking a bite of macaroni and cheese and chewing, "you've never told us about your life in Chicago. What do you do there?"

What did he do there? Good question. The past year, he'd taken care of his mother. He'd scarcely seen anyone, never daring to leave her alone. One elderly neighbor had come in once a week so he could do the grocery shopping and run errands. He could've hired some help, but his mother didn't want strangers around.

"I was a stockbroker," he snapped.

Another gasp. What was wrong with the woman? This time he glared down the table, seeking Camille out. He discovered she'd closed her eyes, her pale lashes resting against even paler cheeks.

Jake brought his attention back to the subject at hand. "Was?"

"I retired when Mother got sick."

"Retired? You must be a lot older than you look," Pete offered with a chuckle. Several others joined in.

Griffin realized he should've been more guarded in his answer. But it was too late now.

"I got lucky," he said gruffly.

"Lucky with someone else's money!" Camille leaped to her feet after her bitter words filled the air, and she hastily excused herself and ran from the room.

Megan, with an apologetic smile in Griff's direction, followed her.

"What was that about?" Griffin asked.

"I'm afraid Camille just had a really bad experience with a stockbroker," Chad explained.

"She lost some money? Buying stock is a form of gambling. Surely her broker warned her of the possibility?"

"I don't think so," Jake drawled. "People seldom warn you right before they skip town with all your money."

Griffin considered Jake's answer, wanting more details, but Jake wasn't willing to change subjects.

"We can discuss Camille's misery another day. Tonight we need to settle things between us."

"What's to settle, Jake? I don't belong here."

Red spoke for the first time. "Why don't you? You're a Randall, aren't you?"

Griff smiled at the man. "It'd be hard to deny, sitting next to Jake."

"Damn right," Jake agreed with a chuckle.

"But because we look alike, because my mother was raised here, doesn't mean I should live here. I belong in a big city. Where I've always lived."

No one responded, and Griff breathed a sigh of relief. Maybe they understood at last.

"You know, I've never been to Chicago. What's it like?" Jake asked as if nothing important had been under discussion.

Griff was ready to describe his hometown when the door opened and Camille and Megan returned to their places at the table. He watched Camille, but she never looked his way. Murmuring something softly to Red, who sat at the foot of the table, she picked up her fork as if she were starving to death.

"Uh, Griff? Chicago?" Jake prodded.

"Oh, uh, yeah," he replied, hoping his cheeks weren't as red as they felt. "Chicago is big, busy. It's on the banks of Lake Michigan. There are beaches and museums, parks and office buildings. Anything you want."

"Sounds like a fine place," Jake said, nodding.

Griffin nodded. Great. Jake accepted his decision, and he'd be out of here first thing in the morning.

"But Chicago will still be there next week, won't it? I'd really like for you to hang around here a few more days."

Griffin swallowed and took one look at the other end of the table. "Uh, Jake, I—"

"What's a few more days, Griffin? It'll give us all time to get to know each other."

That's what he was afraid of.

GRIFFIN STOOD on the back porch, one arm wrapped around the post that supported the roof, staring up at the night sky. The air was crisp, almost chilly, but no colder than it would be in Chicago. But the stars were incredible.

Nothing interfered with their brilliance out in Wyoming. Too bad he couldn't say the same for life. Jake wanted him to stay a little longer.

Mixed feelings swirled inside him. He felt a kinship with Jake that almost frightened him. He didn't have close friends in Chicago. Not buddies, not someone with whom he shared his deepest feelings. Yet Jake, he knew, could become that kind of friend.

One of the reasons he was anxious to leave the Randall ranch was because of his vulnerability. His mother had taught him to remain apart. To owe nothing. To love no one. The Randall ranch was a quagmire of love.

He snapped his head around as he heard the back door open. To his surprise, Camille drifted toward him in the moonlight.

"I owe you an apology," she said softly.

"You do?"

"I shouldn't have made the remark I did at dinner…about your being a stockbroker." Her words were soft, her tone husky, making him even more aware of her body. She wasn't little; her head topped his shoulders, but he knew she'd fit perfectly against him.

"That's okay. According to Jake, you have some reason to hate stockbrokers."

She didn't answer, and he caught a hint of movement, as if she shrugged her shoulders.

"Did you report your broker to the stock exchange? They have special investigators who—"

"I reported him to the police."

"Poor investments may indicate bad judgment, Camille, but I seriously doubt it's a crime," he protested.

She turned to face him. "He absconded with my fortune, Griffin. It wasn't a case of poor investments."

"You've got proof?"

"Yes."

"Have they found him?"

"No."

"You can't trust strangers, Camille. You should've had some safeguards that would've prevented—"

"He was also my fiancé."

Her words stopped him cold. She'd broken his cardinal rule. Never mix business with anything else. "That was a mistake."

"Oh, really?"

Her response was heavily sarcastic, but he figured he owed her that, at least.

"So what are you going to do now?"

"Get on with my life. I'll have to earn my way now."

"How are you going to do that?"

This time she turned away from him and stared out across the dark countryside, the shadowy Rocky Mountains in the distance. "I don't know yet. That's why I'm here, to take time to figure out what to do. I think I'll find a job, save some money so I can go back to college for an advanced degree. Maybe I'll become a stockbroker." She stared up at him, almost as if in challenge.

"If I can help in any way…" He wasn't sure what he was offering, but he felt compelled to do so. He also felt compelled to touch her. With one hand, he traced her jawline.

Instead of jerking away, she laid her face against his hand, drawing a deep breath. "Thank you. There's nothing you can do."

Her breath feathered his arm, and he was the one to draw back. The moonlight shone on her blond hair and cast shadows over her fair skin. As if it couldn't help itself, his hand reached out again to smooth away a wayward strand of silky hair.

She shifted a little closer as she leaned on the same pole. "Are you really going to stay?"

"Yeah." His voice sounded rusty, hoarse. "For a few days."

"Then you'll leave?"

He couldn't decide if she was relieved or upset about his departure.

He nodded. Then added, "I don't belong here."

She reached up as if to smooth down his collar, but she let her hand fall without touching him. "Why not?"

"I have my own life in Chicago." His hand settled on her shoulder. For all her curves, she felt small, fragile. He moved a little closer.

"How can you be family if you don't see each other? Will you be all alone in Chicago?" Her gaze remained fixed on his chest, just over his heart.

"I have friends." Distant friends.

His other hand wrapped around her back, urging her closer. All along he'd known what he was doing, pulling her closer to him, luring her lips into the danger zone. Now he dipped his head, and his mouth covered hers. Electric shock ran through him as he realized how perfectly their mouths joined, how beautifully their bodies fit against each other.

He shifted and refit his lips to hers, urging hers to open to him, teasing her with his tongue, inviting her to join him. And she did. With a matching urgency that flared in him to meet her. With a heat more intense than the sun. With a fear that forced him away.

"No!" he swore hoarsely.

She almost fell against him, barely catching herself as he pulled back. "What? What's wrong?"

"I just don't want you to get the wrong idea."

Backing away, she tilted her chin and stared at him. "The wrong idea?"

"Don't confuse me with my cousins. They may

all believe in happily-ever-after, but I don't. We shared a kiss, but that's all it was.''

He tried to dismiss the fanciful picture of a flower wilting, but she reminded him of one as she withdrew even more.

Stiltedly, she said, "Don't worry, I won't confuse you with those four. You may look like a Randall, but you're not one.''

He was surprised at how much her words hurt. He'd only been a part of the Randall family for four days, and it shouldn't have mattered if he didn't fit in. But it did.

"What do you mean?'' he demanded, his throat tight.

"I mean you may look like them, but you don't have the most important thing they possess.'' Her jaw hardened and her eyes narrowed. "You don't have a Randall heart, Mr. Griffin Randall. And that's why I'll never confuse you with your cousins.''

She didn't wait for a protest from him, if he'd been able to make one. No, she turned her back on him and went inside.

But he had no intention of protesting. How could he? He knew he was different from those four. And he'd counted himself fortunate.

And he still did.

Didn't he?

Chapter Four

Camille stood on the bottom rail of the corral, her arms crossed on the top rail. She'd missed her riding lessons again. Chad, at Megan's request, had promised to turn her into a cowgirl, but ranch duties had canceled most of her lessons.

Not that she was complaining. How could she when the Randalls had taken her in, made her feel a part of their loving circle...given her time to think?

Only Griffin had been less than welcoming. And she couldn't hold him against the Randalls.

Maybe she'd even asked for his behavior. She still couldn't believe she'd melted into his arms last night on the porch. She'd told herself she wasn't even interested in a man, any man. After Clay had betrayed her so thoroughly, she'd vowed to keep her distance from the whole gender.

Until Griffin.

Was it because he looked like the other Randalls? He'd warned her not to confuse him with Jake and his brothers. She didn't know what had caused the magic, good or bad, that had taken over.

What did it matter? The man wasn't interested. He'd made that clear.

Jake didn't believe he'd leave. B.J. had relayed what Jake had told her. He expected to convince his new cousin to stay. But Camille had her doubts. For all the sizzle Griff's touch brought, his gaze didn't get any warmer. The man had a hot body and a frozen heart.

Not that she cared.

Right.

"Hey, Camille," Chad called from the back of his favorite horse, Smoky, as he rode toward the barns. When he got closer, he explained, "Sorry. I started back on time, but I found a mama and her baby in trouble."

She smiled. Chad, and all the Randalls, worked hard, in spite of the family's wealth. "Don't worry about it, Chad. I understand."

"I know, but Megan wants you to learn to ride."

"But she wouldn't want you to abandon a cow in distress, either, would she?" Camille smiled even wider at him. "So, we won't worry about it."

"You're a good sport— Hey! There's Jake and Griff."

She turned to look over her shoulder. The pair had gone on a tour of the county, leaving the ranch shorthanded, one of the reasons Chad had gotten back late.

Chad called to them, then spurred his horse toward the vehicle.

Camille held on to the rails of the corral, though she wanted to move closer. She was going to have to learn better control. At least until Griff returned to Chicago.

"Camille!" Jake called. "Come on over. How was your riding lesson?"

She turned loose of the rail and began to walk toward them, hoping she'd have her composure when she reached them. "We had to give it a miss today," she said, smiling.

"Too bad. Hey, look, Griff bought a new vehicle. What do you think?"

Grateful for a topic she could handle, Camille turned her attention to the vehicle. "A Range Rover? Very nice." *And very expensive.* She avoided the tall man standing beside the driver's side of the vehicle. "Interesting choice for Chicago."

His cool stare challenged her. "Actually, it's perfect for Chicago. We get a lot of snow."

"Yes, I've heard." She gave an awkward bob of her head. "I'd better go help with dinner."

She turned her back on the three men and hurried to the house. So what if they realized she was retreating? At least she'd live to enjoy another day. Without Griffin.

"I gotta find my kids," she heard Jake say. Then footsteps sounded behind her.

"Toby's not home from school yet," she told him over her shoulder.

"Great. I'll get Caroline and pick him up at the bus stop," Jake said, a big grin on his face.

Camille's smile faded as Jake passed her, but she hurried after him. If she didn't, Griffin and Chad would overtake her. She reached the kitchen just as the phone rang.

Red, occupied at the stove, asked, "Camille, can you answer that?"

"Sure." She reached for the phone. "Hello?"

"Just checking in," B.J. said cheerily.

"Everything's fine. We're starting dinner."

"Are Jake and Griff back?"

"They just came in."

"Well, I'm on my way," B.J. said before hanging up.

B.J. sounded as though she hadn't seen her husband in days. That was the kind of marriage Camille wanted, one like any of the Randalls had. She heard Chad and Griff on the back porch and beat a hasty retreat.

She'd already been warned that the new Randall wasn't a family man.

GRIFFIN TOOK HIS PLACE at the table, but his gaze was fixed on the door leading to the rest of the house. Where was Camille? Was she going to take her place beside him, or ask everyone to move again?

And why did it matter?

"So, you're really going to stay?" Brett asked as he sat down.

"I promised Jake I'd stay a few days, that's all. Then I'll go back to work in Chicago."

Anna, settling Victoria in a playpen, looked surprised. "I thought you said you retired."

"I manage a few accounts, and my own investments, of course, so I didn't really retire." A change of subject seemed a good idea. "Uh, Jake talked to me about looking at the family investments." Griffin hesitated. As he'd hesitated when Jake first brought up that subject. "I'm going to look at them, but I don't think I should handle them."

"Why not?" Anna asked.

He was distracted from his answer by Camille's entrance. She had refused to look at him earlier today. Which told him she hadn't forgiven him his rejection on the porch.

He should be glad. He hadn't come here to complicate his life with a woman.

"Uh, I don't think I should make financial decisions for family. Emotions and business don't mix well."

He shifted slightly as Camille slid into her place beside him.

"So are we still going to look at old man Haney's place?" Chad asked.

Jake, entering the room, his arms locked with B.J.'s, answered the question. "We'll look."

"I don't remember meeting him at Mother's service. Was he here?" Griffin asked.

Pete, already at the table after putting the twins in the playpens, said, "Naw. He doesn't socialize much. Keeps to himself. Used to be a good rancher, but I think he's lost heart. His wife died thirty years ago, and they never had children." His gaze shifted to the twins, a smile on his face. "Thanks to Jake, we don't have that problem."

Janie groaned. "Let's don't get carried away. Jake tried to match you up with Megan. Besides, the twins were already on the way when he got his matchmaking idea."

"Hey, I've always been ahead of the game," Pete replied, a big grin on his face.

Janie slapped his arm and settled in beside him. "Quit bragging. I had to drag you to the altar."

"Not true. I dragged you. And I've never regretted it for a minute," he assured her, his gaze fixed on Janie's rosy cheeks.

"Look at Pete. He couldn't stand up to Janie if he tried," Brett teased.

Anna came to rest a hand on her husband's shoulder. "You mean you would go against me?"

"Aw, sugar, never."

The room erupted into laughter.

"Guess I'm not alone," Pete suggested.

No, he wasn't alone in adoring his wife and kids. All four Randalls seemed happy. But Griffin wondered what would happen if one of these women walked out. Or rejected her man, like his father had rejected his mother. Margaret's decision never to risk her heart again had been drilled into him all his life.

As soon as thanks were given, they passed the platters of food around. Everyone was eating and sharing the events of the day, when Chad suddenly snapped his fingers. "Hey, Griff, have you figured out how you're going to spend your days?"

"You mean I have to work the few days I'm here?" he teased, surprising even himself. He guessed the Randalls were rubbing off on him. "I thought I'd just look around. Nothing more specific than that."

"I really need a favor," Chad said, offering a big grin. "I promised Megan that I'd show Camille how to ride, but I keep missing our sessions because of problems on the ranch. Could you give her lessons while you're here?"

"No!" both Camille and Griffin exploded.

Chad frowned as everyone at the table stared at the pair of them.

"I don't want to take up Griffin's time," Camille hastily added.

"And I don't know your stock. I might put her on something inappropriate," Griffin said. Damn. Just what he needed, spending time with Camille.

"I can show you which horses to use," Chad assured him. "And from what Pete says, you're better handling horses than any of us. Must be those Randall genes." He took a bite of food as if everything were settled.

Jake leaned toward Camille. "You'd better take

the opportunity, Camille. I bet Griffin is a good teacher. And he won't be here long, since I can't convince him to stay.''

Griffin turned to look at her struggle for an answer. You'd think she wanted nothing to do with him. And maybe she didn't. But she sure hadn't kissed him like she hated him, he reminded himself grimly.

''Um, we'll see. If—if Griffin has time and I'm not needed here at the house.''

Griffin told himself to keep silent. But he didn't. ''What do you do with yourself all day long?''

Four ladies jumped to Camille's defense. Jake held up his hand, and three of them were silent. But B.J. said, ''She's been invaluable. I'm busy with my animal patients, Anna with her female patients, Megan with her store in town, even though it's only open half a day, and Janie does all the paperwork for the ranch, as well as riding out when they need her. *And* we have a few babies to take care of.''

''Sounds like you're busy,'' Griffin said, arching one eyebrow in Camille's direction.

She kept her gaze on her plate and nodded.

''That's why I wanted her to have riding lessons. She should have some fun while she's here,'' Megan added.

He watched Camille smile at her step-sister.

''You know I'm enjoying myself, Megan. I love all the babies, and you've all become like my family. I can't thank you enough.''

"Shoot," Pete said, smiling kindly, "you don't have to thank us. We're the lucky ones."

There was a general assent before everyone turned their attention back to their dinner. Griffin, somewhere in that conversation, had decided that he would teach Camille how to ride. Whether she liked it or not.

CAMILLE HAD DISCOVERED, upon her arrival at the Randall ranch, that cowboys got up early. And all the babies took after their fathers.

But when she cuddled sweet Victoria in her arms as she fed her her morning bottle, or helped Elizabeth and Caroline get ready for the day, giggling with them when they tried to dress themselves, she never regretted the loss of sleep. Even Richard and Russell were still baby enough to enjoy hugging.

Only Toby had reached the macho stage. But at night, he liked to listen to the stories someone read to the babies each evening.

Before her father's death and her fiancé's betrayal, life had seemed so simple. She'd expected to be a wife and mother, to spend her days as she had since her arrival here. The idea of a career hadn't really entered her mind.

Now she was faced with earning a living. The other night she'd suggested she might become a stockbroker, with the intent to shock Griff. But the idea was gaining in her thoughts. At least she would be a trustworthy one.

Until she made up her mind, or wore out her welcome, however, she was going to enjoy the warmth of the Randall family and take each day as it came.

So she faced the morning with a smile, reaching the kitchen after all the men had left. Or that's what she thought.

"Morning, Red, Mildred," she said, coming through the door with Victoria in her arms. Anna had had an early call shortly after rising.

"Morning," Red sang out, and Mildred smiled.

Then a deeper voice repeated the greeting. "Morning."

She whirled around, and baby Victoria's eyes widened at the sudden movement. "What are you—? I mean, aren't you riding with the others?"

Griffin was sitting at the breakfast table, a cup of coffee in front of him. "Nope. Jake suggested I take it easy. Said I should start giving you lessons instead of spending all day in the saddle."

"No! I—I have to help with the children. Megan can't manage all of them by herself." She gulped air as she turned away.

"Come on and sit down, Camille," Mildred ordered, carrying a plate to the table. "And after, I can take care of Torie."

"It's not just Torie. Everyone's busy except for me and Megan."

"We'll go when they take a nap. Babies do still take naps, don't they?" Griffin suddenly asked.

"Don't you know?" she returned, her tone slightly superior.

"I've never been around babies before," he admitted.

She hadn't, either, until she arrived at the ranch, but she wasn't about to tell him that. "Yes, they take naps, but Megan has to go to her shop this afternoon."

"What kind of shop?" Griffin asked.

"Interior design. She—"

"We'll be around this afternoon, Camille," Red interrupted.

"But you already have so much work to do."

"Jake and I were talking this morning. We're hiring some more help for the house and the babies. Mavis Benson and her sister Ethel are going to come in to clean."

Camille fought to keep her smile bright. "That's wonderful. I was wondering how you'd manage after I leave."

"Hey, we're not pushing you out the door," Red returned. "But you deserve some fun. And that's not possible while you're trailing after the babies all the time."

"When do these ladies start?" Griffin asked.

Camille had almost forgotten about his presence as she realized her justification for staying on at the ranch had just been taken away from her.

"They're coming tomorrow, so we'll leave the heavy cleaning to them," Mildred explained. "We can keep an eye on the babies while they nap and Toby's at school. You can have your riding lesson."

"Thanks," Camille muttered.

The grin on Griffin's face was victorious, as if he'd known she didn't want *him* teaching her. Determined to get her own back, she set little Torie down in his lap, surprising him.

"You don't mind holding Torie while I eat, do you?" she cooed.

The laughter that welled up in her helped relieve some of her stress. The man couldn't have looked more surprised if she'd handed him a rattlesnake.

"But— I mean, I don't— What do I do?" he asked desperately.

Mildred and Red exchanged a glance and said nothing.

Camille worked at portraying a look of calm, though she watched Griffin out of the corner of her eye. She wasn't about to endanger Torie, even to get back at the difficult man.

"Why don't you put her on your shoulder and pat her back. She just had her bottle." She watched those big hands maneuver the baby to his shoulder. He patted gently, as if afraid he'd do some damage.

Torie, who was hiccuping, suddenly got rid of the bubble in her tummy, and some of the formula, as well. The sour smell that emanated from Griffin's shirt was most satisfying to Camille.

"Oh, I'm sorry. I should've given you the cloth to put on your shoulder. Let me help you," she said, jumping up and taking the baby from him, carefully wiping those smiling little lips. "Poor Torie," she cooed, ignoring the man.

Mildred, with a sharp look at Camille, crossed to

Griffin's side. "That's one of the difficulties with babies, Griffin. You'll probably want to change your shirt. Just toss it in the laundry room."

After he left the room, a disgusted look on his face, Mildred smiled at Camille. "I hope you know what you're doing, young lady. That's not how to lead a man down the garden path. You let the babies spit up on him *after* you marry him."

Camille beamed back at her. "Exactly. But since I'm not interested in garden paths, I think I'm okay."

Red poured Mildred and himself cups of coffee and joined Camille at the table. "True. But I think you're going to be in that cowboy's power when you start your riding lesson. So watch out."

She hadn't thought of that.

TWO O'CLOCK.

Griffin checked his Rolex again. He'd told Camille to be at the corral at two, so they could have their lesson.

There was no sign of her. If she stood him up—

The back door opened and she appeared. He watched her walk to the corral, grateful there wasn't a slew of cowboys about. They'd stampede over his body for the opportunity to put their hands on this little lady.

And he had every intention of avoiding touching her.

"Well, I'm here," she said stiffly when she reached his side.

"Right. And almost on time."

She glared at him. "One of the babies needed to change her clothes. She spit up. You know how that goes, don't you?"

The little witch was reminding him of his awkwardness this morning. Well, now the shoe was on the other foot. He was the expert this afternoon.

"How far did you get with Chad?"

She swallowed and looked away. "He—he showed me the equipment, and we petted some horses."

"That's all?" he asked, frowning.

"I—I haven't been around horses much." She paused, then took a deep breath. "At all, actually. I lived in Denver."

"So, I lived in Chicago, and I learned about horses."

Her chin came up. He almost smiled as he watched stubbornness fill her features. "I wasn't interested."

"But you are now?"

"I thought, since I was here, it would be a good thing to learn, but if you think I can't, if you don't want to teach a raw beginner, well, then, I'll—"

"I promised Chad and Jake I'd teach you." Under his breath, he muttered, "I just didn't realize how much I had to teach."

"What did you say?" she demanded, her features stiff with pride.

"I was trying to figure out where to start our lessons," he said coolly, hoping she didn't question him further.

"Oh."

He opened the corral gate. "Come on in here and I'll introduce you to the horse Chad recommended."

He promised himself he hadn't intended it. How was he to know she was so green she didn't know to watch where she should step. When her boot came down in a pile of manure, however, he couldn't resist.

"Oh, I'm sorry, I should've warned you. That's one of the problems with horses. Kind of like babies," he added with a big grin.

Chapter Five

She had to leave.

Camille scooted farther down into the steaming water, allowing her muscles full access to the heat. Her head needed some relief, too, she decided, as tears filled her eyes.

She didn't want to leave. The Randalls were so wonderful, welcoming her, treating her like family. She hadn't felt so centered, so whole, in years.

As long as she'd felt she was contributing, she hadn't thought about leaving. But now, with the two ladies coming in to help, they wouldn't need her.

And then there was Griffin.

She winced as she shifted her legs in the steamy water. It was his fault she was indulging in the decadence of a bath in the middle of the afternoon. Megan had taken one look at the way she walked after her lesson and immediately insisted on the hot bath.

It was also his fault that she had to leave. She might've been able to find something else to do to help out around the house. But she couldn't find a way to avoid Griffin Randall, no matter how she tried. If the Randalls thought there was a problem, they'd want to fix it.

And today had made it very clear she had to avoid him. Especially his touch. Not that he'd intentionally lingered with his hands. No, after the first time, he'd tried to avoid her as much as she tried to avoid him. Because something happened when their skin came into contact.

Lightning.

Tornado.

Earthquake.

Or something very similar. Something neither of them wanted. After he'd helped her clean her boot, he'd led her to the placid animal Chad had chosen for her to ride. He'd explained about mounting the horse. From two feet away.

Camille, however, didn't quite grasp the essentials. After placing her foot in the stirrup, which seemed awfully high to her, she tried to step into the saddle, as Griffin had said. Gravity got the better of her, however.

Griffin to the rescue. He had molded her hips in his large hands and pushed her up, almost across to the other side. Fortunately, he'd taken her gasp as alarm that she might fall.

She knew differently.

That recognition of desire filling her, enticing her to slip back into his arms, frightened her more than the horse did. What was wrong with her? She knew now was not the time to even think about a man.

And Griffin had made it clear that even if the time was right, he was the wrong man.

A knock sounded on the door. "How are you doing, Cammy?" Megan asked. The use of her childhood nickname touched Camille's heart.

"Fine, Megan. Do you need me?"

"No, the babies are sleeping. When Anna gets home, she'll give you a massage. That will help."

"I'll be all right. I'm just not cut out for horseback riding." That was her only hope. If she could stop the lessons, maybe—

"Don't be silly. Everyone feels that way at first. Now more than ever, you need lessons every day."

That was what she was afraid of. Camille closed her eyes again. "But I don't have time—"

"Nonsense," Megan said briskly through the door. "All you've done since you got here is work. It's been such a relief to the four of us," she said, referring to the Randall wives, "but we want you to have some fun, too."

Fun.

That wasn't how Camille would describe her contact with Griffin. "Well, I'll be leaving soon, anyway, Megan, so I won't have time to—"

"I don't want you to leave, Cammy. Stay just a little longer. We won't work you so hard."

"Megan, I love playing with all the babies. I never had brothers and sisters. It's been fun."

"I know, but— Oops, there's one of the twins calling. I'll check on you in a minute."

Maybe a minute would be long enough to come up with a reason to avoid Griffin Randall.

GRIFFIN HAD REMAINED at the barn after Camille's riding lesson. The smell of hay calmed him. And he needed calming…and time to think.

He was an experienced man. Because his mother had preached at him to avoid love didn't mean he hadn't had relationships. But always on his terms. He'd always been in control. He'd always been up front with the women with whom he'd been intimate.

With Camille, he wasn't in control.

And he certainly didn't intend to tell her that. When a man lost control, a woman thought she gained it. That wasn't going to happen.

As long as he could avoid touching her again. Because something happened when he touched her. A powerful hunger seized him, a hunger to feel her flesh, to bring her body against his.

After he got her on the horse, he'd retreated, stepped back, done his teaching through words. He'd put her through a grueling hour, not knowing if he was trying to punish her or himself. At the end of the lesson, she couldn't even dismount alone. She would've fallen on her face.

So he'd moved to her side, giving her his strength as she'd slid off the saddle. Her body, in those sexy jeans, had slid down his, lighting it up like a pinball machine everywhere she touched. Her scent filled his nostrils, and his arms had tightened around her.

He'd considered picking her up. But he knew he would have headed for a clean pile of hay rather than the house. He'd have removed every inch of clothing she wore, until nothing was between them.

What was it about Camille Henderson that attracted him more than any other woman? She was beautiful, of course. But he'd had beautiful women. She could be charming, her smile warm and tender, her eyes lighting with humor.

Stop! His body was reacting predictably. He didn't want to— The sound of horses increased his need to avoid showing any reaction. These men might be his cousins, but he wasn't about to reveal his vulnerability to anyone.

After a deep breath, he moved out into the sunshine. Jake was the first to arrive, greeting Griffin with a big smile.

"Everything all right?"

"Fine," Griffin muttered. He offered to take care of Jake's horse, but his cousin refused.

The other three Randalls arrived together.

Chad immediately got to the heart of Griffin's problems. "Did you give Camille her lesson? How did it go?"

"I'm afraid I overdid it, Chad. I don't think I'm the right person for the job. How about I ride out with the others tomorrow and you stay here and give her a lesson? I think she'd prefer that."

He watched Chad look at his three brothers, silently communicating something. He wasn't sure what.

"Well, we'll see. But I planned to take a couple of the boys and comb the foothills, in case we missed any of the cattle in the roundup we just finished. You wouldn't know where to look." He unsaddled his horse without looking at Griffin.

"Wouldn't your hands know where to look?" Griffin was feeling pretty desperate to avoid Camille.

"Not like me," Chad assured him with a grin. "I've been riding those foothills all my life."

"Pete, you could come with me," Griffin suggested. "That would free up one of the cowboys to do something else."

Pete cocked one eyebrow. "I'd enjoy that, Griff, but tomorrow I'm getting a new gelding for the rodeo string. In fact, I was hoping you'd be around to help me with him."

Griffin eagerly leaped at the opportunity to be busy with something else besides Camille. "Sure. I'd be pleased to help. Camille will understand I've got to help you."

"Oh, that won't be a problem. The animal will be here in the morning. You'll be free for the afternoon riding lesson."

Griffin felt his stomach sink. Then Jake approached and put a hand on his shoulder. "We really appreciate you giving Camille the lessons. She's had a rough time lately, what with her father's death and that skunk of a fiancé."

Griff frowned. "Did he wipe her money out completely?"

"Just about. We want her to have some fun, especially since she's been helping the girls out since she got here."

Griffin knew when he was trapped. He gave up without any more protesting. "Glad to help out," he muttered, and picked up Brett's saddle and bridle while the cowboy started brushing down his horse.

"I'll get that in a minute," Brett protested, but Griffin didn't stop.

"I don't have anything else to do. No problem."

So he walked away, missing the grins the four Randall brothers shared. After all, they recognized misery when they saw it. They'd all been there, done that and survived to march down the aisle.

CAMILLE HAD CONSIDERED remaining in her room for supper, using her soreness as an excuse, but she realized that was not an option. She would have the four Randall ladies hovering.

And she couldn't ask for a different seat at dinner without throwing the spotlight on her and Griffin.

She entered the kitchen with Megan just as everyone was sitting down. Griffin stood by the end of the table, waiting for her to sit.

"Are you all right?" he asked softly, leaning toward her after taking his place.

She stiffened, trying to deny the sizzling sensations that filled her. "Yes."

"I was afraid you'd be sore. I may have pushed you too hard this afternoon."

"Anna gave me a massage." She tried to keep

her answer to a minimum. She didn't want an intimate conversation with the man beside her. That wasn't true. She didn't want an intimate conversation with the man beside her about horseback riding. Her cheeks flushed as she admitted to herself how interesting another kind of conversation might be.

"Are you running a fever?" he asked.

She glared at him. "No!"

"Everything all right?" Jake asked, leaning toward the two of them.

"Fine!" they snapped back in tandem, then glared at each other again.

"How did the riding lessons go?" Jake persisted, his gaze sharp.

"Fine," they repeated together, but their animosity was carefully banked, so their response would sound normal.

Camille suddenly realized everyone at the table was staring at them. With a bright smile, she said, "I didn't know horses smelled so—so strongly. I may carry some perfume with me tomorrow."

Smiles and chuckles came in response and several general conversations began, which eased the embarrassing moment. She took a deep breath and shifted away from Griffin's lean, hard body. She would control her reaction if it was the last thing she did.

She hoped her words weren't prophetic.

The phone rang. Mildred, closest to it, got up from the table and answered. "Yes, he's here."

Every man in the room looked up. She held out the receiver and said, "For you, Pete. Long distance."

Dinner continued, though Camille thought most everyone was listening to Pete's call with one ear. When he hung up the receiver, he was glowing with enthusiasm. "Janie! I've been asked to deliver a speech at the rodeo conference next week. They had a last-minute cancellation when Don Gay got sick."

His wife stood and gave him a hug. "That's wonderful. You're finally being recognized for the good job you do. I'm so happy for you."

"Even better. You haven't asked where the conference is." He waited for her to do as he suggested.

"Well?" she prodded.

"Hawaii!" He swept her up and spun her around, then slid her down his body for a kiss.

Camille looked away, knowing their visible love would only increase the hunger she felt.

Everyone at the table began talking about Hawaii, and the pleasure Pete's visit would bring.

"You're going with him, aren't you, Janie?" B.J. asked.

"I'd like to, but with the twins—"

"Don't be silly, girl," Red interrupted. "We've got you covered. You don't want to turn that boy loose on a beach with women wearing those little bitty bikinis. He might forget to come home."

Janie grinned, but it was Pete's response that settled everything. "I don't want to go if you're not going with me."

"But, Pete, think about what you're saying,"

Janie urged. "This recognition will make a big difference to your business."

He squared his jaw, giving that stubborn look that all four Randalls—maybe five, Camille amended as she glanced at the man beside her—had perfected.

"Nope. Not without you."

Camille spoke up. "I'm going to have to leave soon. So you should take advantage of my being here, Janie. You deserve a vacation. In fact, I think you should all go."

There was a shocked silence that was suddenly filled with voices as the four couples discussed her suggestion.

When Anna suggested she and Brett stay at home, he protested. "Nope, I'm not going to permit it. If anyone should go to Hawaii, it's you." Then, he looked up and down the table. "We weren't going to tell you for a while, but Anna's pregnant."

"But Torie's still so little," Mildred said in surprise, then closed her mouth as her cheeks reddened.

"We didn't plan to— I mean, it just happened," Anna assured everyone.

"Hell, Anna," Jake protested, "you don't have to explain to us. We're happy for you. Besides, I agree with Camille. Everyone should go, if Camille, Red and Mildred think they can manage."

"A'course we can. After all, without all you hungry galoots to cook for, I'll have a lot less work," Red argued. "There'll just be four adults and the five children. Torie don't eat enough to count."

"I could go back to Chicago, making it one less

for you to worry about,'' Griffin offered with a smile.

Camille thought he looked relieved at the idea of leaving.

''Actually, Griff,'' Jake said, ''I was going to ask you to keep an eye on things at the ranch while we're gone.''

Camille watched a trapped look fill Griff's eyes. She glared at him, because she wanted this vacation for the Randalls.

Finally, he looked at Jake. ''Sure. I'll be glad to help out.''

''Then that settles it,'' Jake said with a grin. ''Pete, make reservations for eight. We're going to Hawaii.''

''MILDRED, DON'T FORGET Torie likes her juice at ten each morning.''

''Camille, the boys' favorite story is Pooh Bear,'' Janie added to Anna's reminder.

''If Caroline cries, give her her lamb,'' B.J. said. ''She always sleeps with it.''

''And Elizabeth likes oatmeal for breakfast,'' Megan chimed in.

''Like I don't know that,'' Mildred muttered as she stood beside Camille on the porch. ''Go on, get out of here,'' she then shouted in mock anger. ''We've seen these children before.''

Camille smiled at the understatement. Mildred had been on the ranch since before the twins were born. All morning the Randall wives had been offering bits of needless information in between packing and hugging their children.

Toby had been glad to leave for school after a litany of dos and don'ts from his parents. From Griff's look of fellow sufferer, Camille suspected he'd been receiving warnings and suggestions about the ranch work from the male contingent of Randalls. He was urging his share of the vacationers into his new Range Rover. Red was going to drive the others in the family Cadillac.

"Well, it's time to be on our way," Jake announced, and Camille sent up a silent prayer of gratitude. She and Mildred waved goodbye, each holding a tearful twin. The three little girls were napping.

"The hardest part is gettin' rid of 'em," Mildred announced after the cars left the yard.

"Yes, it was. I had no idea they'd be so upset." All four women had had tears in their eyes as the cars pulled away.

"They'll recover. Like the boys. It's just that they haven't left them before. This trip will be good for all of them."

"I hope so."

Richard tugged on her face, his pudgy hand demanding attention. "Read a book?"

"Sure, sweetheart, let's go read a book, and maybe Mildred will fix us a snack while we read. Okay, Russell?" The other twin nodded, and Mildred set him down. Richard joined him, and they both clutched Camille's hands. With a grin at Mildred, Camille led her charges up the stairs.

She was content. At least until Griffin was back on the ranch.

Chapter Six

Griffin and Red got back in time for supper. Griffin had been amused at the turmoil involved in sending the family off on their vacation. But he noticed the difference when he came out of his room, after washing up.

"Can you give Torie her bottle?" Camille asked without looking up.

"I've never done that. I might mess up."

Red smiled as he stuck a spoon into Elizabeth's open mouth. Camille was feeding Caroline, and Mildred was supervising the twins.

"It's the easiest job, boy. Better take it before you get stuck with those two." He pointed to the twins.

Toby came to Griffin's rescue. "I'll show you how."

"Thanks, Toby," he replied, though it was embarrassing for an eight-year-old to know more than him.

Toby showed him how to heat the bottle and then test its warmth. "Next, you have to pick her up. And support her head. Mom always says that's most important.''

"How?" Griffin couldn't have been more nervous if he'd been asked to be featured tenor at the Met.

Camille put down the spoon she was using and handed each little girl a biscuit to occupy her time. Then she came over to the playpen where Torie was fussing. Bending over, she scooped the baby into her arms with ease.

Griffin stood admiring her, from her perfect behind, shown off when she bent over, to her ease with the baby. Then she thrust the child at him.

"Crook your arm," she ordered, then laid the baby against him. "Keep her head higher than her feet and put the bottle in her mouth. There's nothing to it."

Toby handed him the bottle, grinning. "You can sit down, if you want."

Griffin moved slowly to the table and settled himself, then offered the bottle to Torie. She fussed and reached for it. Between the two of them, they finally guided it to her rosebud lips.

He sighed with relief as she concentrated on the milk, realizing Red was right. This job was easier than feeding the more active children. He grinned when Elizabeth grabbed the spoon as Camille guided it to her mouth, dumping the mashed potatoes on the tray of her high chair with a splat.

"You won't be laughing when it's your turn," Camille muttered.

"I think I'd better stick with Torie. You know, work my way up," he teased.

"Exactly. Torie eats baby food before she takes her bottle. You didn't get here in time tonight."

"You mean with a spoon? Can she chew?"

"Mercy, yes," Mildred assured him. "She's got four teeth. But baby food doesn't require chewing."

Toby leaned against his shoulder and whispered, "The peas are the worst. They look like—"

"Toby Randall! Don't you dare use that word at the dinner table, or you'll be eating with the babies instead of the adults," Mildred warned.

"Daddy said it first," Toby announced, his jaw squaring like his stepfather's.

"But Daddy didn't know you were listening, Toby, and he apologized to Mom for saying it, didn't he?" Camille reminded gently.

"Yeah."

She offered the little boy a smile, its warmth like a caress that had Toby smiling back at her. Griffin could understand his reaction. He'd give a lot for a smile from Camille. She'd scarcely spoken to him since their time on the porch.

He received instructions, and a cloth to cover his shoulder, for burping Victoria before he put her in her own playpen. The four toddlers were settled in the other playpens, where they would entertain themselves while the adults and Toby had their own dinner.

"Will they have to add another playpen when

Anna has their second child?'' Griffin asked, staring at the setup.

"I reckon they'll start with a bassinet, then a crib like Torie uses now," Red explained. "And the twins are about to outgrow that playpen."

"I thought it would be Janie and Pete who added to their family first," Mildred said, her brow creased. "I hope Anna is recovered enough for a second baby. We're going to have to keep an eye on her."

Red nodded in agreement. "Yep. Torie will only be fourteen months when the second one is born."

Griffin noted the concern in their eyes. He discovered Camille, too, was frowning. "Is anything wrong with Anna? I mean, I know she's small, but—"

"Naw, and she's a midwife. She's knows all about birthing. You just can't help worrying. Sometimes, I think we have so much happiness around here, something has to go wrong by the law of averages," Red said with a sigh.

"I hope not," Camille said fervently. "They deserve their happiness."

"Right," Mildred agreed. "We're just being worrywarts. Eat your dinner. I want to get the dishes cleaned up before the babies tire."

Camille joined Mildred in doing the dishes. Griffin discovered that meant he was on child patrol. Not too difficult since he and Red sat at the table with a cup of coffee and watched them play.

"I like the division of labor here," he said with a grin.

"Don't be countin' on things being so tame, youngster," Red warned him. "Sometimes, tears just won't go away."

"What do you do then?"

"Pray the women know the reason," Red said.

"Ah." He'd pray, all right. Pray that they all kept so busy that Camille stayed far away from him.

AFTER THE CHILDREN were all in bed, Mildred and Red settled in front of the television.

Camille slipped out to the back porch after donning a jacket. Now that she'd realized she would be leaving soon, she wanted to savor every moment at the ranch. The Wyoming night, with its star-filled sky and crisp night air, was a pleasure.

The back door opened, and she spun around to discover Griffin stepping outside. She knew he wouldn't seek her out, so she figured he hadn't known she was there.

"Aren't you cold?" he asked.

"I have a coat on."

"Yeah." After a silent pause, he said, "You really took on a big load."

"What?"

"Offering to take care of all the children. It's a big job."

"It's not like I offered to do it on my own. Red and Mildred are wonderful, and you're even pitching in in the evenings." He'd been a lot better than she'd expected. "Besides, it's fun. I always wanted brothers and sisters. Didn't you?"

There was a long silence. Then he said, "Why would I wish my misery on someone else?"

She held her breath. "Your misery?"

She saw him give an attempt at an indifferent shrug in the darkness.

"My mother was a bitter woman. I kept trying to make her happy, and I couldn't."

"No. It wasn't your responsibility."

"But—"

"Listen to me. I'm an expert on this subject. I went to a therapist once a week for several years after my mother died. I thought it was my fault she went away."

"Surely you knew better than that?"

"I was only ten. We'd had an argument and she sent me to my room." She couldn't believe she was revealing this secret. "She left to run an errand, while the housekeeper kept track of me. A drunk driver hit her. She never came back."

She hadn't realized he'd moved closer until his well-muscled arms surrounded her and she was cradled against his chest. She should protest, but she didn't. Instead, she enjoyed the comfort he offered. The comfort she'd sought for and never found with her fiancé.

"The psychologist told me over and over again that I wasn't responsible for her accident or her happiness. And you weren't, either," she emphasized, slipping her arms around him.

Instead of his being comforted, too, he broke away from her. "My situation was different."

"Why?"

"It doesn't matter. I think it's getting colder. You'd better go on in."

Anger rose in her. He thought he could order her about? "I don't want to go in. And I don't want to be dismissed like I'm a child."

"It's for your own good."

"I'm not going to catch a cold."

"Damn. I tried," he muttered. Then she was swept back into his arms, and his lips covered hers.

HE KNEW BETTER. Griffin had warned himself after the horse riding lessons. Touching her was a problem. He'd tried to tell her to go inside.

His lips caressed hers. His arms traced her curves through the jacket and jeans. His mind was spinning out of control.

Not that she was protesting. Her arms were around his neck, her fingers surging through his hair. She moved against him, as if afraid he'd go away.

Not likely. No man could walk away from such a temptation. His hands settled on her hips, which fitted perfectly into his hold. He pressed her even more tightly against his arousal.

"Hey, Camille," Red called from the back door, "I— Oops!"

Camille pulled away at once, her gaze flying to the back door. "Y-yes, Red? Did you need something?"

"Naw. I thought you might be interested in a program on television, but—but I guess not," he added, a low chuckle in his voice.

Camille's cheeks weren't the only ones that reddened. Griffin was grateful for the shadowy darkness on the back porch.

"I'll go back to Mildred. Just forget I interrupted."

After Red disappeared as rapidly as he'd intruded, silence fell between them. Camille continued to stare at the back door, as if waiting for something.

Griffin finally spoke. "Now do you want to go inside, like I suggested?" If she didn't, he feared he'd sweep her back into his arms, and that wasn't a good idea.

She spun around and glared at him. "Don't you dare pretend what happened was my fault, Mr. Griffin Randall. I didn't invite you to—to…grab me!"

"Ha! You put your arms around me."

"You already had your arms around me! I was only trying to reassure you that your mother's unhappiness wasn't your fault."

"Don't pretend some sob story made you kiss me," he grated, regretting his openness. Pity wasn't what he wanted from her.

"Me kiss you?" She shoved at his chest. "You kissed me!" Before he could protest—and he intended to—she admitted, "Okay, I kissed you back, but I'm not the one who started this."

He felt like beating his head against the post. "Shh! You'll wake the kids," he cautioned, "or at least have Red appearing again.'' They'd both been yelling. Probably the entire county had heard their heated words.

She drew a deep, angry breath. In a deadly whisper, she said, "I'll be quiet. I'll be so quiet you won't even know I'm here."

The witch he still wanted to kiss swept around him like a grande dame in Victorian times, her nose in the air. If it were Victorian times, she'd be banned from society for her wantonness.

And he wanted her back in his arms.

He stood there in the cold, wishing he were anywhere but here, this close to temptation.

GRIFF DREADED returning to the house the next evening. He hadn't seen Camille at all that morning, but his night had been filled with dreams of her. In the dark loneliness of his bed, he'd carried their embrace to its logical, and in his opinion rightful, conclusion. In his mind.

And woken up frustrated.

When he came in for supper tonight, everything was calm efficiency. Camille avoided looking at him, but she accepted his help feeding the horde.

Griffin was amazed at how well everything was going, in terms of the children. Not that he contributed a lot. The others tried to spare him since he'd been out on the range all day. But he helped.

What amazed him most of all was the love the three adults showed the little ones. Their patience seemed endless. And a lot of patience was needed at bath time. But Griffin couldn't hide his laughter when the twins created a tidal wave and he and Red were splashed.

An hour later, the house was silent. Griffin discovered he needed a change of shirt after the bath hour. He'd just shrugged into his shirt when there was a knock on his door. He opened it before buttoning up, thinking Red had something to tell him. Instead, Camille stood there, her gaze fastened on his chest.

Tension immediately flowed between them. Griffin hurriedly began buttoning his shirt, feeling overexposed as Camille's cheeks flamed.

"Yes?" he snapped.

"Oh. Um, telephone. Butch wanted to check with you about tomorrow." She whirled around and rushed back into the kitchen.

He followed, thinking about her words. Butch. Butch was a good-looking cowboy, one of Jake's most trusted employees. Griffin liked him.

But he didn't like the casual way Camille said his name.

"Butch? Griffin here."

They discussed the plans for tomorrow. Griffin felt everything was taken care of. He was about to hang up the phone when Butch said, "So how's life at the big house with the beautiful Camille?"

"Fine." The beautiful Camille? It wasn't that he didn't think she was beautiful, but he didn't like hearing that Butch had noticed, too.

"I had plans of asking her out until everyone left.

Now I suppose she won't have time for socializing until they get back.''

If Butch was asking him to fill in for Camille so she could spend an evening with him, he was barking up the wrong tree. "You're right. Too many babies."

"Why don't you call her back to the phone? I'll make plans for after their return."

Griffin was an honest man. At least he'd always thought so. Until now. "She's already gone to bed, Butch. It's been a long day."

"Hell, it's only nine o'clock," Butch protested.

"Babies sap one's energies," he returned coolly. "I'll be glad to give her a message."

"No, I'll talk to her tomorrow. Earlier."

"Fine. I'll see you in the morning." He hung up the phone, a satisfied smile on his face.

Until he turned around and found Camille staring at him.

"Who's gone to bed?"

"Uh, I thought— That is, you disappeared after coming to get me, so I thought you'd gone to bed."

"Butch wanted to talk to me?" Camille looked puzzled. "Why?"

Griffin groaned. Did the woman have no idea how attractive she was? "He wanted to take you out," he admitted, anger filling his voice.

"Now? I can't go anywhere until everyone returns."

"That's what I told him."

She tilted her head to one side. "You thought I wouldn't know to tell him that?"

"Of course you would. I was just trying to help out." He hoped she bought his lame excuse, because he'd run out of reasons. Other than the truth.

And he really didn't want to admit that he was jealous as hell.

With a shake of her head, she changed the subject. "Red and Mildred are in the den and asked if we wanted, I mean, if you wanted to watch *ER* with them. It's just starting."

"Sure." Anything to get him out of the conversation about Butch.

And he'd try to keep Butch so busy tomorrow he couldn't think about a certain blond beauty. Griffin frowned. Keeping busy hadn't worked as an antidote for him. But he'd think of something, because Camille and Butch together wasn't something he could accept. And he didn't bother asking himself why.

Chapter Seven

Griffin was in the barn, grooming the horse he'd ridden that day. He'd spent a lot of time in the barn since the Randalls' departure three days ago. It was safer. He looked up in surprise to see Camille enter. She'd stayed as far away from the barn as possible. "Something wrong?"

"Yes." As he dropped the grooming brush and moved toward her, she held out her hands, palms out, to stop him. "Wait! I didn't mean— There's no emergency. Well, there is, but not here."

"Something's happened in Hawaii?" he demanded, his face reflecting his concern. There had been telephone calls every day from the vacationing parents.

"No, it's Mildred's cousin."

Griffin stared at her. Had he missed something? "Mildred's cousin? Do we know Mildred's cousin?"

Camille shook her head and gave a helpless shrug. "No, we don't. But she's fallen and broken her hip. She needs Mildred to come take care of her."

"But the babies—"

"Two people can handle them. With the food all prepared and the two ladies coming every day."

"Oh," he said with a sigh of relief. "So you and Red are going to cover? I'll try to come in earlier, then. I've been—I mean, I thought it would be better—" He broke off and shot her a look of frustration. She knew what he meant whether she acknowledged it or not.

She didn't bother pretending not to understand. "I know. That's why I have to ask you this before you come to the house."

"Ask me what?"

"If you'll help me take care of the babies."

His eyes widened. "You just said you and Red could handle everything."

"Griff, Red wants to go with Mildred. And she needs him to go. They're distraught at being separated. It wouldn't be too hard, if you're willing. Parents manage a lot of kids all the time. And the cooking and cleaning wouldn't be a problem. You'd have to give up riding out with the cowboys, but I think they can manage until the guys get back."

"What did Red say?"

Camille seemed puzzled about his meaning. Then she said, "I didn't say anything to them about Red going with her. I wouldn't, not until I talked to you." After a pause, she admitted, "It will mean us being together all day. You've already indicated an aversion to my company...."

He groaned, staring at her. "You know why I

don't want to be in your company. I'm trying not to lead you on. I'm returning to Chicago after the guys get back. But I'll admit to a powerful attraction when I'm around you.''

''Okay, consider me warned. You're leaving. Is that the only problem?'' she asked, thrusting her chin in the air.

''Damn it, no! *This* is the problem!'' He grabbed her and pulled her into his arms, lowering his mouth to hers.

Camille should have been used to the effect of his touch on her, but she wasn't. And she wasn't sure she ever would be.

Just as she thought she'd never think again, she was suddenly thrust away from his warmth.

''That's the problem!'' Griffin muttered, glaring at her.

''So, we promise not to touch each other,'' she snapped, trying to sound firm when her insides were all aquiver. ''It seems selfish to let our difficulties keep Red and Mildred apart. Besides, she's going to need Red to help lift her cousin. According to Mildred, she's, uh, large.''

Griffin raked his fingers through his thick dark hair. Finally, he looked at Camille. ''All right, you win,'' he conceded with a sigh. ''We'll take over for them, but you'll have to tell me what to do. I'm not experienced with children, like you.''

She grinned. Obviously, she was a good actress, since she'd only been caring for children for the past few weeks. But she wasn't going to reveal her inexperience now. "Great. Can you come to the house with me now, to tell them? Mildred's getting ready to make travel arrangements. That way they wouldn't have to make them twice."

He rubbed his chin, shaking his head. Then he turned back to his horse. "Let me finish taking care of Alberta," he said, picking up the brush and returning to his work.

"Alberta? That's the horse's name?"

"Yeah. Jake said she came from Alberta, Canada." He grinned over his shoulder. "I felt kind of funny calling her that at first, but I'm used to it now. She's a good ride."

Camille stepped closer and rubbed the mare's nose as Griffin brushed her. It was a pleasant moment, a sharing, which hadn't been a pattern of their acquaintance.

And it would probably be the last peaceful moment they would have for the next few days.

ANOTHER GOODBYE.

Griffin and Camille stood on the back porch and waved goodbye to Mildred and Red.

Camille smiled and assured the worried couple they'd be fine. Her insides were trembling again, but she wasn't about to show her fears.

Griffin put his arm around her, and she froze. Surely he wasn't going to break their promise already?

"Well, Ma, it's just you and me now. Think we can make it?"

"Ma?" she asked, staring at him in surprise.

He grinned at her. "It just seemed appropriate."

She hadn't seen much of his lighter side, hadn't even been sure he had one. She couldn't hold back a return grin. "Okay, Pa. I think we'd best get back inside before the Indians attack the wagon train."

He turned to walk inside with her. "Any smart Indian would run in the other direction. Five babies! At least Toby is old enough to talk to."

"He's also old enough to go to school. You go wake him up while I fix breakfast. Then you'll need to drive him to the bus stop today."

Red and Mildred had wanted an early start. The sun wasn't even up yet, but as the pair entered the house, Camille could hear Torie already crying. "Oops, I guess I'll make breakfast after I see about Torie."

"Whoever gets to the kitchen first will make breakfast," Griffin amended.

"You can cook?"

"You'll be surprised what I can do."

She went in the opposite direction when they reached the top of the stairs, glad she didn't have to react to his innuendo. She'd already been amazed...every time he touched her.

An hour later, when he left to drive Toby to the bus stop, she sat at the table watching the twins feed themselves while she spooned cereal in Elizabeth's and Caroline's mouths. Torie had gone back to sleep after her early bottle.

"Richard, do not throw food at your brother."

His only response was a grin before he blew bubbles of oatmeal at her.

"I need to sound more like Pete," she muttered to herself. She turned back to the girls, realizing the boys were going to have to have a bath anyway.

"Young man, no! Do not put cereal in your hair," Griffin ordered from the back door.

She was glad to see him. And to her surprise, Richard had halted his criminal activity. She was about to congratulate Griffin when Russell looked around expectantly.

"Daddy? Daddy?"

Griffin's gaze met hers in consternation before he knelt beside the little boy. "Sorry, Russell, it's just me, Griff. Daddy and Mommy will be—"

"Mommy?" Richard called. "I want Mommy!" Suddenly, the oatmeal was mixed with tears, first Richard, and then Russell.

It took about thirty seconds for the little girls to join in the crying. Breakfast ended in a shambles as they tried to console the children and clean them up at the same time.

Finally, Camille decided to resort to a Disney video. She carried the two girls and Griff took the boys. All of them settled on the couch after she put in the video. After fifteen minutes of *Cinderella,* the children forgot their crying and watched the mice and birds and old hunting dog.

Griff breathed a sigh of relief. "I guess I owe you an apology," he whispered.

She looked over the children at him. "Why? It's not your fault you sound like their daddy."

He gave her a one-sided grin that made her want to caress his cheek. "Maybe I should sound like that fat mouse from now on."

She couldn't hold back a chuckle. "Just as long as you don't try to look like him."

"Why, Miss Henderson, don't tell me you wouldn't appreciate me if I were roly-poly? Surely you can't be so shallow?"

Her gaze roamed his sexy body, and she found her throat dry. Looking away, she tried to keep her voice even. "Of course not."

Before he could tease her any more, they both heard Torie stirring through the baby monitor they'd brought along with them.

"Uh-oh. Can you keep an eye on them while I get Torie and feed her some breakfast?"

"I don't think I have a choice. Go ahead, we'll manage."

And manage they did. All day long, between the two of them, they cared for the children. When the girls napped, Griffin took the twins to the barn to visit the horses. Camille thought she would have a minute to herself then, but Torie woke up, fussing.

"What's the matter, sweetheart?" Camille asked. She tried to make the baby happy, talking to her, giving her her favorite toys, but Torie was not her happy self.

Griffin returned with the twins, looking for a

snack he said the twins wanted, but she noted he didn't turn down the cookies and milk she offered.

Later they prepared dinner together, thawing out some of Red's meat loaf, and after the children had eaten, Griffin suggested it was their turn.

"You're hungry already?"

He grinned at her. "I think baby-sitting is harder than cowpunching."

"I think you may be right." She served the two of them while he transferred the children to their playpens.

"Is that why you stayed?" she asked as they began eating.

He looked up, frowning. "What?"

"Is that why you stayed instead of returning to Chicago right away? To punch cows?"

For a moment, she didn't think he would answer her. Finally, he shook his head. "I stayed because Jake convinced me I should."

"Why?"

"He said we were family. Family should stick together."

"That sounds like Jake. I don't know a man more concerned with family. But you're still going back to Chicago?"

Griffin stiffened. "I belong in Chicago. My life is there."

"You could work here. With all the computer developments, you wouldn't have to be in Chicago to work the stock market, would you?"

He gave her a hard stare. "There's no reason to move here."

"But you could if you wanted to, couldn't you?" she persisted.

"Yes, I guess I could if I wanted to."

She wasn't going to let him off the hook so easily. "So why don't you want to?"

He didn't look at her, his concentration seemingly on his food. "I'm a loner. I'd be uncomfortable in the middle of a big family."

Camille thought about her lonely existence before her arrival at the Randall ranch. She'd been an only child, so her only family member had been her father, since her mother's early death. She'd accepted her life as normal. But once she'd been enveloped in the warmth of the Randalls, the family of Randalls, she knew there had been a void in her life that she hadn't even recognized until it was filled.

Even though she knew Griffin wouldn't appreciate her interference, she had to make her point. In a low voice, she said, "If you leave, you'll be giving up something most people would give anything for."

"What?" His frown made it unlikely he really wanted to know, but she answered him anyway.

"Family. A warm, loving family. The Randalls are special."

He put down his fork. "I'm a Randall by name. That's all."

She couldn't hold back a grin. "Have you looked

in a mirror lately? You're a Randall by blood, for sure."

His sexy lips slipped into a half smile. "I guess I can't deny that. Some of the cowboys even forget and call me Jake."

"That's a high compliment."

He seemed to recall his earlier stance. "But that doesn't mean I belong here."

"It's a start."

"Look, Camille, I have a life. A perfectly good life. And when they return, I'm going back to Chicago to get on with that life. They may be family by blood, but I'm not a part of their lives and they're not a part of mine."

Toby, who'd been watching television, wandered back into the kitchen. "Uncle Griff? Will you help me with my homework when you finish eating?"

"'Uncle'?" Griffin demanded harshly, frowning.

Camille held her breath, wanting to reassure Toby, but realizing any such words would have to come from Griffin.

Toby looked apprehensive. "Are you too busy?"

"No, Toby, I just— I hadn't heard you call me Uncle before."

"Aren't you my uncle?"

The child's innocent question summed up their discussion, and Camille waited for Griffin's response. Whether he intended it or not, his days on the ranch had made him a part of the Randall family. She suspected, even if he went back to Chicago, he would take memories of his visit with him that he would never forget.

To Camille's relief, he gave that dazzling Randall smile to the little boy. "I'm not sure I'm really your uncle, but you can call me that if you want. And I'll be glad to help you with your homework."

"In fact, why don't you get your books, while I clear the table," she suggested. "We've about finished, and you two can work here while I do the dishes."

"Thanks, Camille." Toby hurried out of the room.

Later, after Toby's homework had been dealt with and the children bathed and put to bed, Camille poured cups of decaf for the two of them. A mellowness had invaded Griffin after their earlier conversation, leaving her eager to talk to him again.

Griffin had gone to his room behind the kitchen to check the markets on his computer. He intended to sleep in Jake and B.J.'s room upstairs until the others returned, but most of his belongings were still in the other room.

"Griff?" she called.

"Yeah?"

"Coffee's ready, and I've cut us both a piece of cake."

"The chocolate one?"

"Yes."

"I'll be right there."

He joined her almost before she sat down. She grinned. "You must really like that cake."

"It's good. And I seem to need a lot of calories to keep up with all the kids. They're sweet, though."

"Yes, they are."

"Do you want—? I guess that's a silly question," he said, and took a big bite of cake.

"What?"

"I was going to ask if you want kids, but it's obvious."

She nodded. "I'd like to have four children."

He almost choked on his cake. "Four?" After a sip of coffee, he said, "Four's not politically correct, Camille. The world is overpopulated, or haven't you heard?"

"I've heard. But my children will be loved and provided for. I don't think the world is overpopulated with those kind of children." She raised her chin and stared at him, daring him to contradict her.

That elusive grin reappeared. "You could be right. But maybe you could have two of your own and adopt two others?"

"Maybe. But I'm not having only one, whatever I do."

"You've thought all this out, haven't you?" he asked with amusement.

She gave a tired sigh and looked away. "I thought I was going to marry."

To her surprise, he reached across the table and clasped her hand. "I'm sorry. I didn't mean to bring up bad memories."

She said nothing, but he continued to hold her hand. Then he said, "You'll marry, I'm sure."

Attempting to add a dash of levity, she added, "Yeah, but not to a Randall. After all, you're the only single one and you've made it clear you're not staying."

He didn't laugh. "Exactly," he snapped, a frown on his face. "There are lots of other men around. The Randalls don't have a corner on happy marriages."

"True," she agreed with a tired sigh. "But they seem to understand the importance of family, of trust, of—of true love."

"And it doesn't hurt that they're wealthy and handsome," he added with sarcasm.

She stared at him solemnly. "You know, when I first came here, I might have agreed with you. They're all you said and more. Just as you are. But it's their values that are the real catch. A woman wants more than a handsome face. She wants to know that her husband will be there tomorrow, no matter what it brings. She wants to know that he'll always love her, that he'll never intentionally hurt her."

She'd had enough. It had been a long day. "But, as I said, I'll have to look elsewhere." Then she stood. "I'm going to bed now. The children will be up early."

"Camille—" he began, but she was already at the door, and she didn't wait to discuss her future anymore. Certainly not with him. Because he wouldn't be a part of it, which happened to make it look pretty bleak.

IN SPITE OF her early bedtime, Camille hadn't gone to sleep right away. When she finally did fall asleep, it was deeply. So deeply, in fact, it took several minutes for Torie's crying to awaken her.

Panicked, she shoved back the covers and ran for the baby's bedroom without even turning on any lights.

And ran smack into Griffin, bare chested, rumpled sweatpants the only clothing he wore.

His arms shot out to keep her from falling, and she shivered. "The—the baby!"

"You thought I was out for an evening stroll?"

She ignored his sarcasm, opening the door to the baby's room. The night-light seemed too bright after the darkness, but it showed baby Torie clinging to the side of her crib, crying.

"Oh, sweetie, it's all right," Camille hurriedly assured the baby. Picking her up, she cuddled the little girl against her.

"Damn it, Camille! Don't you own a robe?"

Camille turned to stare at him. He was standing there bare chested, chastising her for not wearing a robe? "I was in a hurry," she said. "You don't have one on, either."

"No, but I'm not standing in front of a light in a little piece of material that reveals more than it conceals!"

Chapter Eight

The woman was driving him crazy! All day long, he'd watched her cuddle the babies against her breast, smile, laugh, love the children.

And he was jealous!

Now she was standing before him practically naked and didn't even realize it.

But he did.

With flushed cheeks, she squared off at him, Torie clutched to her shoulder. "Don't look!"

"How can I help it?"

"I don't need you here. Go away. Then you won't be bothered."

Her chin was in the air, which, he'd already learned, meant she was in her stubborn mode. She might not be blood kin to the Randalls, but she had that particular Randall trait mastered.

Her words also showed how little she understood the male psyche. Like he would be able to forget her tempting body just because he wasn't in the same room with her.

Or the same state.

He pulled his stare from her, upset at how reluctantly he did so. "Do you want me to get a bottle for Torie?"

"No! You might think I was trying to seduce you when I took the bottle." She glared at him.

"Camille, I didn't mean—"

"What makes you think I'd *want* you to marry me?" With a sniff that she tried to hide by turning away from him, she added, "I don't have any money left to attract a man, so I think I'll manage on my own."

He couldn't remain across the room. In seconds he'd crossed the space between them and wrapped his arms around the woman and child. Rocking her head back against his shoulder, he soothed her attempt to pull away. "Cammy, sweetheart, any man who only wanted your money, not you, is a fool. He threw away the most valuable thing."

Another sniff. "You don't believe that."

"Oh, yeah, I do. Just because marriage isn't for me, doesn't mean— All four of my cousins believe it. Isn't that enough? Can't you see how much they believe in the relationship they have with their wives?"

"Yes. So why can't you believe it?"

He stiffened.

She lifted her head and stared into his eyes. "Please, I'm not suggesting you marry me. But— I've watched you. You fight against believing in love and marriage. And yet you expect me to believe?"

His breathing grew labored. How could he answer her? "I want you to believe. I want you to have what my cousins have."

"But you don't believe it will last?"

His hold around her tightened, as if by holding her close he could convince her. "My mother taught me feelings weren't reliable. I do well in the stock market because I never let my feelings intervene. I analyze, I use logic, I reduce everything to fact. I never use gut feelings, like some people."

He swallowed, fighting the warmth flooding him as he pressed her against him. "Feelings are transitory. They don't last. As happy as my four cousins are now, in five years they could be ripped apart, children separated from one parent or the other, anger, animosity where love once was."

"No!" She buried her head in his shoulder, and Torie whimpered. "Don't even say such a thing. I won't believe it. It won't happen."

His lips caressed her temple, and he inhaled her scent. He wanted to deny his own words, but he couldn't. He'd been taught too well. "Cammy, there are no guarantees."

She lifted her head and stared at him, her blue eyes flooded with tears. "You're wrong, Griffin Randall. If there ever was a group whose marriages won't fail, it's your cousins. They'll beat the odds."

"Why? What makes them so different?" He wanted her to convince him, to give him facts that made a difference.

"Because they love each other more than themselves. I've seen all of them put the other first, do chores for the other even though they were tired. Reach out for each other when there was need. I've seen it!''

"And when one of them stops?"

"They won't! They won't!" she almost shouted, and Torie, feeling the tension, whimpered again.

So there they were. No facts. Nothing to analyze. Just emotion. And he didn't trust emotion. "I'll go get Torie's bottle," he muttered, and stepped away from the warm bundle he'd held.

And felt an immediate loss.

He hurried out the door to the kitchen, where he could concentrate on material things, like bottles, dishes, food. Anything but feelings.

CAMILLE OPENED HER EYES the next morning to find two little boys staring at her. "Richard, Russell, what time is it?"

"Breakfast," one of them announced with a happy smile.

She checked her watch to discover she'd overslept, something that seldom happened with kids. "Oh, Toby has school. Go wake up Toby, would you, guys? And I'll get dressed and start breakfast."

"Breakfast," one of the twins repeated—Richard, she thought. Then they ran from the room.

Camille grabbed jeans and a shirt and scrambled into them. No time for a shower now. As soon as she tied her tennis shoes, she sprinted for the door.

Time to do a quick check on Torie, Elizabeth and Caroline before she went downstairs.

It occurred to her that she should awaken Griffin, but after their midnight confrontation, she dismissed that idea. All three girls were still asleep, which surprised Camille. When she reached Torie, she leaned over to tuck the cover a little closer to her baby cheeks and felt a warmth that seemed excessive.

She ran her hand over the baby's head and recognized fever, even as inexperienced as she was.

"Oh, no!" Her decision not to awaken Griffin was immediately thrown out. "Griffin?" she yelled as she picked up the baby and headed toward the door.

He met her in the hallway, his eyes wide with shock. He was bare chested again. "What's wrong?"

"Feel her," she insisted, hoping he would tell her she was wrong about Torie's fever.

Puzzled, he reached out a hand. "She's hot. Do you think she has fever?"

"Yes. I'm going to call the doctor. Can you get Toby up for school? I sent the twins, but they—"

"I'll manage," he assured her, turning her in the direction of the stairs. "Go ahead."

A quick conversation with Doc Jacoby took some of the panic away, but suddenly all the experience Camille had gained in the past few weeks seemed woefully inadequate. She was so afraid she wouldn't be able to care for little Torie.

She searched the shelves and found the baby Tylenol. Then she fixed a bottle of water, dropping the medicine into the bottle so the water turned pink.

All the movement had awakened Torie, and she was complaining. Her mewling sounded a lot like her behavior last night. Camille suddenly panicked, wondering if the baby had been sick last night, but she and Griffin had been too involved in their own difficulties to notice.

The sound of boots tumbling down the stairs reminded her that Toby had to be sent off to school. When Griffin and the three boys came through the door, their first thoughts were of Torie, not breakfast.

"What did the doctor say?" Griffin asked. His concerned look was reflected in Toby's gaze.

"I'm giving her medicine, and Doc is on his way. He said it probably wasn't anything serious." She tried to smile, hoping to reassure them, but she felt the smile wobble around the edges.

"I can't go to school if Torie's sick," Toby said, his brows knitting together. "You might need me to help. Sometimes I hold her."

Griffin and Camille exchanged a look before he knelt down beside the eight-year-old. "You are a terrific help with Torie, Toby, but Doc says it's not serious. And you know your mom expects you to be in school."

"But—"

"After school, I'll be waiting for you to come home," Camille told him, "because you'll be able to relieve me by rocking her. So don't get too tired at school.''

"Okay. I'll skip recess today so I'll have energy," he solemnly assured her.

Camille couldn't help it. Toby might not be much for hugs but he was getting one now. "You are such a terrific boy, Toby Randall." She even kissed his cheek.

When she released him, he looked at Griffin, his cheeks red, and protested. "Girls."

"Yeah," Griffin said in sympathy. "But she's right. You're a good man, Toby."

The boy ducked his head, and Camille did what she could to relieve his embarrassment. "Time for breakfast. Could you guys eat cereal this morning? I don't have—"

"I'll take care of breakfast," Griffin said. "You take care of Torie."

Much to her amazement, he began frying bacon, while Toby, with the doubtful assistance of the twins, set the table. Toby even filled the small, roly-poly juice glasses the twins used with orange juice. Then he buttered toast as it popped up.

Camille set in the rocker, cuddling Torie and trying to get her to swallow the water, and watched the menfolk take care of the food. Then, just as Griff was scrambling eggs, she heard one of the girls.

"Oh, Toby, could you check on the girls? I think they're waking up. Just bring them down here in their pajamas. I'll help them dress later," Camille instructed.

The little boy raced upstairs. A couple of minutes later, as Griffin was putting the eggs on a plate, Toby reentered the kitchen, holding each little girl's hand.

"I don't think Caroline feels good," Toby whispered to Camille as he approached her.

With shaking fingers, Camille reached out to touch Caroline's flushed cheeks. "Oh, no. Griff?"

He looked up from the stove, distracted. "Yeah?"

"Caroline's sick, too." She tucked the bottle for Torie under her chin and reached out to hug Caroline.

Griff quickly settled the three boys at the table, with Toby in charge of the twins, then put Elizabeth in her high chair.

"Do you think it's the same problem as Torie?"

"I don't know. Doc should—" Camille heard a car drive up. "Maybe that's him now."

She'd met Doc Jacoby at church, so Camille recognized his cheerful face as he entered the house without knocking. "We're glad you came, Doc."

"Easier than having you gather all these young'uns up and come to the office. How are we doing?" he asked as he approached Camille and Torie.

"We seem to have two sick ones. Caroline is running a fever, too, we think." She nodded her head toward the little girl cuddled in Griffin's arms.

Doc pulled up a chair next to the rocker and extended his hands for Torie. "We'll start with this little one and then we'll get to Caroline."

Camille hoped Doc was okay working with an audience. Even Elizabeth stopped eating her toast to watch him examine her cousin.

"Well, now, little girl, you're going to be just fine," he muttered, and Camille breathed a sigh of relief.

"It's not bad?" she asked.

Doc chuckled. "Oh, it's going to be bad for you two. Torie has chicken pox. She's going to be mighty fussy before it's all over. And so will the rest of them. Toby, you had chicken pox in kindergarten, didn't you?"

Toby frowned. "I think so. Is that when you get bumps all over your body?"

"That's right."

Camille remembered her own childhood bout with chicken pox and shuddered. "What can we do to help them?"

"There's a special oatmeal bath you give them twice a day. Calamine lotion will help ease the itchiness, too. Mittens will keep the little ones from scratching too much." He paused and looked at her and Griffin. "Mostly, you just have to wait it out."

"Should we call their parents? I hate to ruin their vacation," Camille said.

"Naw, no need to do that. You got enough help here?"

"Yes, we have two ladies coming every day to clean, and Red cooked a lot of meals and froze them. We should be all right."

Griffin didn't sound as sure. "Do you mean *all*

the kids are going to come down with chicken pox?''

"Well, now, Toby shouldn't, though I've heard of some kids getting it twice. But the other five probably will. Looks like Torie's having a light case of it, but you never can tell. I've seen kids get scabs in a lot of strange places, even inside their noses.''

"Don't you think I should stay home and help?'' Toby asked anxiously.

Camille held her breath, hoping Doc would deal gently with the little boy's concern.

"That's a mighty nice offer, Toby, but the babies are mostly gonna sleep. Your mom will want you in school. Then when you get home, you can help these two.''

Griffin stood, handing Caroline to Camille. "Finish your breakfast and I'll drive you to the bus stop. We might even let the twins ride with us, since they're not sick yet.''

"We'll need the bath stuff and lotion for the girls, Griff,'' Camille reminded him.

"I'll get someone from the drugstore to bring out what you need,'' Doc suggested. "We can just put it on the regular bill.''

With a nod of acknowledgment, Griffin rounded up the three boys and headed out to the truck.

"There's coffee already made, Doc. Would you like a cup?'' Camille offered.

"Don't mind if I do. No, stay down, I'll get it. This little lady is just about asleep,'' he added as he stood and placed Torie in the daybed, tucking her blanket around her. "Can I get you a refill?"

"Yes, please."

He returned with two cups of coffee.

Caroline, too, was falling asleep, and Camille laid her down. Then she turned her attention to Elizabeth, still gnawing on a piece of toast. As she cut up some banana for the little girl to eat, Doc asked, "So, what do you think of the newest Randall?"

Many answers went through Camille's mind. Finally, she chose the most innocuous. "He's a fine man. Quite like his cousins, in spite of never having met them until recently."

"He sure looks like Jake, don't he?"

"Yes, he does."

"I remember Margaret, his mother. A strongheaded little lady if there ever was one. Spoiled by her daddy. She cut a wide swath through the men when she reached puberty."

Camille offered a polite smile in return but said nothing. She was uncomfortable discussing Griffin and his mother.

Doc didn't seem to notice her unease. "Yeah, she was real popular with the men. Though not with the ladies. Her pa couldn't see that she was hurtin' anyone. He held Gus to a much higher standard."

"A lot of fathers favor their daughters."

"Yeah, but they exercise a little more discipline than her old man did. It sure caused everyone a lot of heartache in the end. Has Griff said who his daddy was?"

She looked up, surprised by the question. "No. I don't think he knows."

"Does he want to know?"

"Doc, you'll have to ask Griffin that question. We haven't— I mean, we aren't— We haven't discussed things like that."

"You're right, of course. Maybe I'll wait until Jake gets back before I speak to Griffin."

"Do you know who he is?" she asked, suddenly realizing the significance of his questions.

"Maybe. There were a few rumors. And hindsight is always better. We're a small community here, you know."

"Yes. I think you're right. Wait for Jake's return. Griffin seems to be willing to hang around for a while, so—"

"Juice!" Elizabeth demanded, since Camille seemed to have forgotten her.

"Oh, okay, Elizabeth." She got up from the table to refill the child's glass, automatically checking on the other two, sleeping nearby. It gave her an excuse not to comment on Griffin's plans. As she returned to set Elizabeth's glass on her high-chair tray, she heard the truck returning.

"Griffin and the twins are back. I don't think—"

"No, I won't say anything now," Doc agreed, much to her relief.

From what little she'd heard Griffin say about his father, she didn't think he would be interested in hearing Doc's opinion. Better to discuss it with Jake first.

Griffin entered with a twin on each hip, a smile on his lips, and Camille felt the attraction to him growing. "Did Toby get off to school okay?"

"You bet. These two little monsters cried to get on the bus, too. But I promised them a cookie when we got back to the house. I know it's bribery, but—"

"It works," Doc assured him with a grin. "I wouldn't mind having one of those cookies myself."

"I'm sorry, Doc, I didn't think to offer you one. Griff, could you...?"

"Coming up. Come on, Richard, Russell, you have to sit at the table for your cookie. And I'll pour you some milk."

"Cookie!" Elizabeth declared, not about to be left out.

"I hope our supply lasts until their parents get back," Griff said.

Doc asked about the vacationing Randalls, eager for news, and Camille told him about the phone calls. Then he asked about Red and Mildred, as if he had all the time in the world.

Camille enjoyed his presence. His expertise reassured her that the children were okay. And he provided a nice buffer between her and Griffin. One they needed after last night.

Finally, however, he stood. "Well, I'd best be on my way. You give me a call if you have any questions, Camille," he ordered. "And I'll get some things sent out from the drugstore."

"Thanks, Doc. We really appreciate it."

As he turned toward the door, Griffin halted him. "There's just one thing, Doc."

"Yeah?"

"I think I should tell you I've never had chicken pox."

Chapter Nine

"Lord have mercy, boy, why didn't you say so?"
Doc demanded.

Griffin sighed. He'd debated even mentioning the
fact, because he figured adults didn't catch chicken
pox. "I hoped it wouldn't matter. Can adults get
it?"

"Yes, they can. And it can be a lot more serious
than it is with the kids." Doc came back to Griffin's
side and reached out to feel his cheek, then look
into his eyes. "How are you feeling?"

"Fine."

"Well, listen up. If you start feeling bad, no macho stuff. You hit the bed at once and stay there."

Griffin must've shown his skepticism.

"How serious will it be?" Camille asked, her
eyes wide with concern.

"It can make a man sterile if he's not careful,"
Doc said gruffly, frowning at Griffin. "You hear
me? And call me at once." His last order was directed at Camille.

"I will, Doc, I promise."

Doc said his goodbyes and left. The only noises in the room were the children's. Neither Griffin nor Camille spoke.

"Cookie!" Elizabeth shrieked, reaching for the plate again.

The twins took up her cry, and Griffin looked at Camille. "Do we let them have another one?"

"I don't think it will hurt. After they each take one, put the rest away. Maybe if they can't see them, they won't want any more."

Griffin did as she asked, but he recognized the same theory she'd tried last night. If the kids were as crazy about the cookies as he was about wanting Camille, he didn't think hiding them would work.

Camille suggested he stay in the den with the three that were well, while she cleaned the kitchen and kept an eye on the two that were sleeping.

Griffin did as she suggested, only stopping by his bedroom to get his laptop computer. He could work on his stock portfolio at the same time.

Half an hour later, Camille came to the door of the den. "Everything all right?"

"Yeah, but I need to talk to you."

He'd debated this move almost the entire time since he left the kitchen. A stock he'd been keeping an eye on seemed ready to make a big move. He'd decided to place some of his money in the stock, and some of the Randall Corporation money that Jake had insisted he invest for them. He felt he should do the same for Camille.

But in view of her past experience, he wasn't sure she would trust him.

"Cammy," he began, unconsciously calling her by her nickname, "there's this stock I've been watching. I think it's going to go up quite a bit. I'm putting money in it and, well, I want to invest some of your money, help you get back some of what you lost."

She appeared stunned by his words. "You want me to invest more money in the stock market, after what happened to me?"

"I'm good at what I do. I wouldn't steer you wrong," he assured her. For some reason, it was important to him that she trust him.

Camille had to say no. "Even if I wanted to, I don't have enough to make a difference. Besides, we both know there's always a gamble, even if the stockbroker is honest." She paused but couldn't keep from saying softly, "I do trust you, Griff. I believe you're honest. But I'm not investing in the market again, not unless I'm in control."

"We'll pretend you gave me the money. You can pay me back later if it pans out."

"Griff, no. I won't let you do that."

"Cammy, I'm not your fiancé. I won't lose your money." He reached out to take her hand. "Remember what I said last night? I analyze. I deal in facts. I know what I'm doing."

Camille stared at him. She could use an increase in her financial state, but she wasn't taking pity from this man.

"Thank you, but I don't need charity."

"You're being bullheaded."

She gave him her sweetest smile. "It takes one to know one."

"What can I do to convince you?"

"What can I do to convince you that leaving the Randall family would be a mistake?"

He appeared stunned by her question. "The two have nothing in common!"

"Yes, they do. We each have a prejudice, me against investing in the stock market, you against families." With an ironic curve of her lips, she walked out of the room. If she stayed any longer, she would be too tempted. To trust Griffin, not the stock market.

Griffin stared at the door, willing her to return. But nothing happened. Ridiculous female! Determination surged through him. He'd prove her wrong. He'd set up the account in her name, loan her the money and when it surged, as he expected it to do, he'd prove his point.

Then she'd have to acknowledge he was right...without him having to do the same. His thoughts skittered away from the Randall family and his leaving. Of course he would go. There was no reason to wonder if Camille was right, after all.

CAMILLE REAPPEARED at the door to the den an hour later, having resolved to keep their relationship on a friendly basis. Nothing personal. "The cleaning ladies came a few minutes ago. They've gone upstairs to make the beds and start the laundry, so I'm leaving the other two asleep in the kitchen.''

"Good. In a few minutes, I'll take these three kids outside to work off some energy. Will Elizabeth like that?"

"I think she'll love it. Little girls like going outside, too," she assured him, amused by his uncertainty.

"I've never been around children at all," he said, "so all I have are my own memories to rely on."

"You've adapted quickly, Griff, and I appreciate your help so much. I expect we'll be getting our daily call soon. I hope I can lie well."

He studied her, and she wondered what he was thinking. He soon let her know. "I think maybe I'd better take the calls. You couldn't fool anyone."

"Griffin! I can, too."

"Nope. Are we keeping Red and Mildred's departure a secret, too?"

"I think we should. Don't you? They would only worry. And if you take the call, they're going to wonder why you aren't out on horseback."

"I'll think of a reason."

He didn't have much time. The phone rang. With a smile in her direction, Griffin reached for the receiver. "Hello?"

Camille knew it was the Randalls because Griff smiled at her, nodding.

"Aloha to you, too. How's the weather?"

"Daddy?" Richard asked, crawling from the end

of the sofa, over Russell and Elizabeth to reach Griffin. Of course, as soon as the other two realized what he'd said, they were clamoring to talk to their parents, too.

"Wait, guys. Let Uncle Griff talk," Camille urged, trying to hold them off Griffin.

"Yeah, we're caught up on the chores and I thought I'd take some time to watch a few cartoons. I miss them, you know."

Camille had to admit his casual tones were more convincing than hers would be.

"No, everything's fine here. What could go wrong?" After a pause, he said, "No, he and Mildred ran into town to do a little shopping. Camille's here to make sure I don't do anything wrong."

"Griff!" she protested, her arms full of two little boys and Elizabeth. "Oh, look, there's Bert and Ernie!" she exclaimed, drawing the children's attention back to the television.

Fortunately, her trick worked.

"Whatever you want to do, but there's no need. We're all fine here."

Camille looked at Griffin. Were they thinking of coming home early? She hated to admit to herself how much better she'd feel if they did. Today was Tuesday and they weren't due home until Sunday.

When he hung up the phone, she asked him when they were returning.

"They were talking about coming Friday, but I told them we were fine. They haven't decided."

"We're not going to be fine if you get sick." There. She'd admitted the fear that was building in her.

"I probably won't get sick, Cammy. I'm a big boy. If I do, I'll just take it easy."

"If you do, you'll go to bed at once, like Doc said."

"Lady, you're not big enough to make me." He squared his jaw, the way all the Randalls did.

"Griff, surely you wouldn't take a chance on—on becoming sterile. You're so good with the children, you should have some of your own." She'd even dreamed of his children, though she'd never admit that to him.

He shrugged his shoulders. "If I never intend to marry, I probably shouldn't have children anyway."

"That's your choice, but I want it to be a choice, not a decision made for you by your stubbornness."

A knock at the back door had her jumping up. The deliveryman from the drugstore arrived. Camille tipped him for his trouble, then opened the bags. Doc had sent the oatmeal-bath packages. Two dozen of them.

Camille wondered if he thought they'd need that much, but she figured better safe than sorry. Then she found the note.

This should be enough for a couple of days. When you need anything more, call the drugstore. Doc said you can bathe them in the oatmeal stuff as much as you want.

A couple of days? They'd all be shriveled up by then.

TWO DAYS LATER, as she placed another order on the phone, Camille remembered her earlier thoughts. Yes, she felt like her hands were shriveled up from bathing so many children, but the baths soothed their irritated skin.

First the bath, then dotting their bumps with calamine lotion. Only Richard had not fallen from the ranks yet. He was upset that his twin didn't feel well. He tried to get Russell to play with him, and Griffin took him in his arms, trying to explain the difficulty.

Griffin had been a real trouper, pitching in everywhere, from cooking to cleaning up. Elizabeth had come down with it that first night after Doc's visit, even losing her dinner. They had both been so exhausted that night, they'd fallen into bed, separate beds, as soon as the children were asleep.

Which was a good thing, because they'd been up and down all night with fussy babies.

"We'll have this right out to you, ma'am," the clerk said. "You need anything from the grocery store? We could stop on our way."

"Thank you, but no." That was the joy of a small community, Camille realized. She would miss it when she had to return to Denver.

"Did you get the order placed?" Griffin asked as he came into the kitchen, Richard in tow.

"Yes, and I even ordered some new storybooks," she added for Richard's benefit.

"But Russell is sick," Richard said.

"I know, sweetie, but tonight he'll want to hear a new story with you," she promised.

"We're going to go see the horses again," Griffin explained, rolling his eyes.

"Russell loves horses, too," the little boy said.

Griff bent over and swept the three-year-old into his arms. "I know, and when Russell is well, we'll take him to see the horses again. But he needs to sleep now, after his bath."

"Me have a bath, too," Richard told Camille, looking very proud of himself.

"That's good." She leaned forward. "Ooh, you smell good, Richard."

"What about me?" Griffin teased. "I've had a number of baths this morning." His baths had been secondary, given him by the occupant of the tub, but at least he was smiling.

She leaned forward to smell him as she had Richard. Instead, Griffin met her halfway, and their lips touched.

"Ooh! Mommy Daddy kiss!" Richard squealed.

His words had them separating at once.

"Um, no, just a friendly kiss," Griffin hurriedly said, as if he feared even Richard would mention marriage.

"Go to the barn," Camille ordered, irritated with the man's phobia.

As soon as the two males left, the phone rang.

Drat! It was time for the check-in from Hawaii. Griffin had handled the other calls.

"Hello?"

Jake's warm voice greeted her. "How's everything going?"

"Fine. Don't you guys have anything else to do but call home?"

Jake laughed. "It's the women. You know how they hover over those children."

"Yeah, right! It's you, Jake Randall. You can't fool me," Camille assured him with a laugh.

"We've been a little worried since we only talked with Griffin the last two days. We thought maybe he'd run the rest of you off."

Camille attempted a relaxed chuckle. "What man in his right mind would want to be left with six children all to himself?"

"Good point. How are Red and Mildred holding up?"

"Just fine. They're upstairs resting right now. Do you want me to bother them?" She held her breath with her fingers crossed until Jake answered.

"Nope. If they're getting some rest, we'd better not. Are any of the kids around?"

"Griffin just took them on a field trip to see the horses. Except for Toby and Torie, of course."

"Brave man."

"He's been very good with the children, Jake," she hastened to assure him.

"I was afraid he'd be bothered by them. He's not used to children being underfoot all the time."

"He's great with them. I think his voice soothes them because it sounds so much like your voice and your brothers'."

"Good. Well, we'd better go. I'm going to teach B.J. how to surf this morning," Jake said with a laugh, then stopped. "Okay, okay. B.J. wants to talk to you."

Camille tensed. What did B.J. want?

"Camille, I just wanted to be sure Toby wasn't causing any trouble. He's going to school?"

Good. A question she could answer truthfully. "Oh, he's been wonderful, B.J. He goes to school every day and then comes home to play with the babies. He's such a good boy."

"I know. I miss him, and all of them. Paradise is nice, but it's kind of lonely."

"Maybe next time the kids will be old enough to go with you," she suggested. In the distance she heard Torie crying. "Um, if there's nothing else, Torie just woke up."

"Okay. We'll talk to you tomorrow."

She felt sure they would. Rushing up the stairs, she almost ran into one of the cleaning ladies.

"The baby's awake."

"Yes, I heard her, thanks." She rushed into the baby's room to find her standing at the side of her crib. But her color looked normal, and Camille was relieved to discover no fever. And there seemed to be no new spots.

One recovery in progress.

"Good morning, Torie. Are you ready for a bottle?"

She changed her diaper and nightgown, then started down the stairs. Only to be halted by the two other girls' tears.

Reaching for the phone, she called the barn and summoned Griffin. The rest of the day was a madhouse for the two of them. By nightfall Camille thought it couldn't get worse. But it did. Richard had joined sick bay.

GRIFFIN STOOD in the twins' room, looking down at the pair napping in their beds. He was certainly growing fond of Richard and Russell. They were great boys.

All the Randall children were wonderful. He'd never realized how rejuvenating a child's perspective could be. However, with all of them sick, life wasn't going to be quite so amazing the next few days.

At least Toby was still going strong.

Griffin hadn't caught the chicken pox, either. And he had no intention of doing so. He couldn't leave Camille on her own. She was an amazing woman. She never complained or expected to be waited on. He couldn't imagine any woman he'd ever known volunteering to take care of six kids.

He turned and headed back downstairs. He'd start lunch while she settled the others.

Putting some leftovers on top of the stove to heat, he was surprised to be interrupted by a knock on the back door. Turning, he discovered Butch, one of the cowboys on the ranch, waiting.

"Butch, is something wrong?" he asked as he held the door open for him.

"Nope. But I heard about the chicken pox. I thought I should check on y'all. Everything all right?"

"We're fine."

"Camille doing all right?" Butch asked.

Oh, yeah. This was the guy who intended to ask her out. Griffin tried to pretend the tightening of his nerves was for some other reason, but he knew it was really jealousy. "Yeah, she's fine. She's busy with the kids, though."

"I bet. I thought I'd offer my help this afternoon. We're kind of caught up with the chores."

"No, I—"

"Butch!" Camille entered the kitchen. "Nice to see you. Is everything all right?" she asked as she came into the kitchen.

"Well, now, I reckon it's a lot better since you came into the room," the cowboy assured her, a broad smile on his handsome face. "I was just offering to help out this afternoon."

Griffin met her questioning stare with no expression. If she wanted this cowboy lothario running around the house all day, he wasn't going to say anything. Ha!

"That's really sweet of you, and if we had any well ones, I'd send them out with you because they'd have such a good time."

"What about Toby? I've got a couple of chores this afternoon he might enjoy. I'm going to ride out to check on a mama cow and her new baby. Should I wait till he gets home from school and take him with me?"

"Oh, Butch, that's so thoughtful of you. I know he's missed going out with Jake. Do you mind?"

Griff ground his teeth. He could've taken Toby out, if he hadn't been busy with the babies.

"I don't mind at all. And if you think of anything else I can do for you, you just let me know, Camille."

To Griff's horror, she stepped forward and kissed the cowboy on his cheek as she said thank-you.

Butch looked pleased as he left the house. And Griffin couldn't blame him.

"What do you think you're doing?" he demanded as soon as he was sure Butch was out of hearing range.

"What?" she asked as she turned to the stove to see what he'd started cooking.

"Kissing that cowboy! Are you interested in him?" He tried not to sound outraged, but from Camille's expression, he didn't do a very good job.

"Interested in him? I was just saying thank-you."

"Lady, don't you know anything about men? He was offering 'cause he's interested in you. And you just told him you were interested back."

"I did not. I told him I appreciated his offer."

"Oh, yeah? Well, I've done a lot more than offer,

and you haven't kissed me!'' Damn, now he'd done it. He'd showed her how much he wanted her.

"If you'll remember, when we talked about taking care of the kids together, you thought we shouldn't touch."

"Well, I'm changing the rules. If he gets a kiss, so do I!" He pulled her into his arms, and his lips covered hers. And it wasn't some namby-pamby kiss on the cheek!

No, siree, it was a full-fledged, spine-tingling kiss. And then he passed out.

Chapter Ten

Camille grabbed his shirt as Griffin slid down her body. "Griff? Griff!"

No response. He was too heavy for her to hold, so she tried simply to ease him to the floor. Then she hurried to the sink for a cloth. Once it was wet with cold water, she came back to his side to wipe his face.

"Griffin Randall, don't you dare— Come on, Griff, open your eyes!" She almost sobbed with relief when his lashes flickered. As soon as she saw his chocolate brown eyes, she began tugging on his arms.

"Come on, sit up. Are you okay? I don't know—" She stopped as she felt his cheeks and forehead. Even with the wet compress, he was hot. "How long have you been running a fever?"

He blinked several times, like he hadn't awakened yet, then shook his head. "I'm not— I'm just a little warm."

"Do you have a headache?"

"Yeah, but—"

"Come on, you've got to get in bed."

"It's the middle of the day. I'm making stew. I can't go to bed."

"You not only can—you have to," she insisted, still tugging on his arms. "Doc said."

"I don't have chicken pox," he said stubbornly.

"Fine. As soon as Doc agrees with you, you can get out of bed." She tugged again, but he didn't budge. "Please, Griff, for me?"

"You're being ridiculous," he asserted, but he struggled to his feet with her help, then swayed.

"Griff!" she yelled, shoring him up as best she could. "Come on, you have to go to bed. Upstairs!" she added when he lurched toward the room behind the kitchen.

Without even answering, he turned in the direction of the stairs. His compliance scared Camille even more. She switched off the burner on the stove as they went past. There wasn't time to worry about lunch right now.

Once she had him in bed, a task that left her breathing like a marathon runner, she picked up the phone.

"Tell Doc that Griffin Randall passed out," she told the nurse. Her terse words got results. Doc came to the phone immediately.

"How is he?"

"He has fever and a headache."

"Why did he pass out?"

"I don't know, Doc. I'm not the doctor." She didn't mean to be impertinent, but she was upset.

"I can't make it for a couple of hours. Is he breathing okay?"

"Yes. Shall I give him some medicine?"

"Yeah. And see if you can get him to drink liquids. I'll be there when I can."

"Thanks, Doc."

Back down the stairs for medicine and juice.

On the way back up, she scooped up Torie and several of her toys and transferred her to her own crib upstairs.

She needed to keep everyone close together because she was going to do a lot of running back and forth.

Then she returned to Griffin's room. He was huddled into a ball, shivering.

"Griff, I have some medicine. It will make you feel better."

No response.

She sat down beside him, putting her arm under his head. "Come on, Griff, open up."

Her touch got his attention. He opened his eyes and stared at her.

"Open up."

As if he understood the words, if not the reason, he did so, and she popped the pills into his mouth. "Now drink."

She put all the authority she could muster into her voice and held the glass to his lips. He sipped some of the juice. After giving him a small break, she ordered him to drink again and got him to take a little more of the fluid.

Then she placed his head back on the pillow. And surveyed the situation. He needed to be under the covers and comfortable.

That meant his jeans and boots had to come off.

Moving to the end of the bed, she took hold of one boot and tugged until it fell onto the floor. The second boot followed.

Next came the hard part.

After eyeing him carefully, she forced him on his back and crawled onto the bed. Her movements eerily followed her recent dreams as she unfastened the buttons on his jeans.

"Keep your head, Camille," she warned herself.

Getting off the bed, she returned to the end of it and began tugging on the pant legs. That strategy failed. She had to get the jeans past his hips before she could pull them off.

Back on the bed, she straddled him and grabbed the waist of the jeans and tried to slip them below his hips. Her hands grazed warm skin, and she groaned. Suddenly, Griffin thrust his lower body up, toward her.

She gasped, then leaned forward. "Come on, Griff," she said softly, "try again."

Only this time she'd be ready.

Again he thrust up, and she tugged his jeans down, revealing white cotton underwear. Somehow, she hadn't expected a Randall to wear anything else. They didn't need silk bikini underwear to entice a woman.

As he stirred under her again, she reminded herself she was supposed to be standing at the end of the bed, pulling the jeans off of him. Reluctantly, she left the warmth of their connection and discarded his jeans. Then she covered him with a blanket. The soft sigh that escaped his lips was her reward.

"All right, sweetie," she said in her best coaxing tones, "I want you to drink a little more. Okay?" She helped him raise his head and poured more juice down his throat.

It was time to check on her other invalids...and decide what to do.

"Everything all right?" Mavis, one of the cleaning ladies, asked as Camille entered the hallway.

"Well, not quite. Mr. Randall has the chicken pox now."

"What? A big man like him? Well, you've certainly got your hands full."

"Yes. Do you think you and your sister could stay until six this evening? I'm sure Jake will pay overtime."

"Well, I reckon we could, seeing as how you're in a bind. But no later. We got our own families to feed."

"Of course. Thank you. I'll go finish heating up lunch. It should be ready in a few minutes."

It was an hour after lunch, when she was reading to the two little girls, that Doc arrived.

"Anybody home?" his voice boomed from downstairs.

She hurried to the top of the stairs. "We're all up here, Doc."

He huffed up the stairs. "How is everyone?"

She filled him in on all the patients, including Griff.

"You've kept him in bed?"

"It hasn't been hard. All he's done is sleep."

"I'd better check on him first."

She joined Doc in the bedroom Griffin was using just as he awoke.

"What happened? Why am I in bed?" he growled.

"You appear to have the chicken pox. Strange."

"What?" Camille asked, her anxiety rising.

"Well, usually it takes longer to transmit the disease, like a couple of weeks."

Camille frowned. "Oh. Maybe they were all exposed at the same time."

"Now, when would that be? Griffin hasn't been out much around the town," Doc said as he took his pulse.

"What about when his mother was buried? There were lots of people here that day. Maybe one of the children who came with his parents had it."

"Dang it, you're right, Camille. I knew I'd heard of another case recently, though they weren't my patients. It was the Biggers from the other side of the county. The wife was a friend of Margaret's. She brought her grandson with her, and I heard he broke out with pox the next day."

"So now we know why. Will Griff be all right?"

"We have to keep him in bed, even when he starts feeling better. You hear me, Griff? This is important."

"Can't leave Cammy all alone with the kids," he said, almost panting, as if even talking was too much.

"Camille will be just fine. If she isn't, we'll get her some help. But you gotta stay flat on your back. Okay?"

Griff barely nodded, his eyes drifting shut.

Doc stared down at him, then abruptly switched his gaze to Camille. "What was he doing when he passed out? Did he knock his head when he fell?"

Camille felt her cheeks redden. "Uh, no, he didn't hit his head."

"Was he standing?"

"Yes, but I was close by and kind of caught him. I couldn't hold him up, but I helped him slide to the floor." And she hoped Doc didn't ask any more questions.

"Well, I guess you know the drill by now."

"Right." But the familiar drill would change slightly. She wasn't about to give Griffin Randall an oatmeal bath like she did the children. Nor was she going to cover him with lotion, either. Maybe she'd get Toby to help him. Or Butch.

"You holler if you need any help," Doc offered. "I'll come back out this evening after dinner to check on Griff. If you've got some soup or something, you should feed him now. We don't want him gettin' too weak and dehydrated."

When Doc left, she heated up a can of soup and fixed a big glass of lemonade. The children seemed to enjoy it. Maybe Griff would, too.

She had to awaken him again. "Griff? Griff, I need to feed you. Doc said." She hoped mentioning Doc would make him more cooperative.

To her surprise, he didn't resist her at all. In fact, his arms snaked around her and tugged her to his chest.

"Griff!" she shrieked in surprise.

"I've missed you," he muttered, and his lips claimed hers. In spite of the pleasure his lips gave her, she could feel the heat from his fever.

Pulling away, she stared at him. "Are you all right?"

"Mmm-hmm, but you're wearing too many clothes. Why did you get dressed?" His fingers moved to the buttons on her shirt. Fortunately, for her modesty, they were curiously clumsy and unable to accomplish their task.

"Griff, what are you doing?" she demanded, covering his fingers to stop their movement.

"Why did you get dressed? We were doing just fine without all this."

"What are you talking about? I was just here with Doc, remember?"

"Doc wasn't in bed with us!" he protested with a rusty laugh and leaned forward to nuzzle her neck.

In bed with us? The man must be hallucinating. For the smallest second, she let herself join him in the dream before she jerked back to reality. "Griff? You must wake up. Please?"

"Anything you want, sweetheart," he muttered, his lips roving her face now.

"Griff!" He kissed her. "Stop, Griff—" He kissed her again, deeply, almost willing her to leave reality.

She finally realized that her closeness seemed only to be extending his hallucinations, not shortening them. She drew away from him, but she admitted she did so with reluctance. His touch was too enticing.

Standing a safe foot from him, she called loudly, "Griff, wake up," and shook him forcefully.

"Huh?" he muttered, frowning.

She repeated her action until some semblance of sanity returned to his eyes.

"What?" he asked groggily.

"I have to give you more medicine and feed you some soup, Doc said." After a look of incomprehension, she added, "Don't you remember Doc being here?"

"We were alone," he began.

"No! I mean, Doc was here." Her cheeks were as red as his and she didn't have fever as an excuse. But she couldn't handle any more of his dreams. As much as she might crave them for reality. Why couldn't he be so—so close when he was conscious?

After giving him more medicine, she pushed pillows behind him and fed him the soup.

"I can feed myself," he protested in a rusty voice.

"Later, we'll see. Right now you have to regain your strength."

"No, I can—"

"Griffin, either you cooperate with me, or I'll ask Butch to come take care of you."

Her words were inspired because he immediately submitted to being fed like the babies. After he finished his meal, he began pushing back the covers.

"What is it? Where are you going?"

"I have to go to the bathroom," he explained roughly. "Are you going to hold my hand?"

She fought against embarrassment. "No, but I'm going to help you walk to the door and wait for you outside. Okay?"

Since he wobbled as he came to his feet, he didn't argue. Camille slid her arm around his waist and guided him in the right direction.

While he was in the bathroom, she found a T-shirt for him to slip into, instead of his Western shirt. The door opened and she turned around. "Why don't you put on this T-shirt? I think you'll be more comfortable."

"Someone took off my jeans," he said with a frown, instead of answering her.

"Do you sleep in your jeans?"

"No. Did Doc—?"

"No, I did. And I don't want any fussing. Now, let's get you out of that shirt." She reached forward and unpopped the snaps on his shirt, revealing an impressive chest. The man's sick. What's wrong with you? She couldn't be lusting after him now, could she?

Apparently, she could, she realized as her hands lingered on his skin. "I—I'll just slide it off of you," she said, her voice breathless.

Afterward she realized her sleep that night would be disturbed by the sight of the handsome man standing there in his cotton briefs. She wanted to run her fingers through his chest hair, to follow it to the scrap of material that saved his modesty.

"The T-shirt?" he reminded her, one eyebrow quirked up.

Her cheeks flamed as she held the T-shirt out to him. He knew. He definitely knew.

It was time for her to tuck him back into bed and remove herself from the danger zone.

The rest of the afternoon, she stayed as far away from him as she could. After Toby came home, she sent him up to check on Griffin and deliver more lemonade.

"Is he going to be all right?" Toby asked when he came back down with the empty glass.

"Why? What's wrong?" she asked, fear clutching her throat. Had her avoidance of Griff caused harm?

"He can hardly sit up. And he's already back asleep."

She sighed. "No, that's okay. Doc said he'd be tired. We just have to be sure his fever doesn't get too high and he gets some rest. You did give him his medicine, didn't you?"

"Yep. What do I do next?"

She smiled at the solemn little boy. "Why don't you sit down and have milk and cookies and tell me about your day?"

"You mean it?" he asked, his eyes wide.

"I mean it. The girls are playing in the den, Torie's in the bed over there, and the boys are sleeping. Mavis and Ethel will hear them if they wake up."

She served him a snack and sat down for a visit. It was the sanest few moments she'd had since Griff had collapsed.

SHE AND TOBY WERE both exhausted by the time the children went to bed at eight o'clock. Toby then took a book to his room to read for a while before going to sleep.

"Not too late, Toby. You've had a long day."

"I know. It'll be nice when Mom and Daddy come home, won't it?" he said, his face wistful.

"Yes, it will. I bet they will bring you back a present."

"Daddy said he'd bring me a coconut." He gave her a puzzled look. "What will I do with it?"

"Take it to school. No one else will have one."

"Hey, yeah, that's right. Okay. Night, Camille."

"Good night, sweetheart."

The house was suddenly quiet and still. She was exhausted, knowing she wouldn't last much longer. She mixed another large pitcher of lemonade for the morning and took more food out of the freezer to thaw out overnight.

Griffin hadn't eaten much dinner, even though the chicken pot pie was tender and tasty. He might need more food, but she figured he had another need or two that she couldn't meet.

Crossing to the phone, she called the bunkhouse and asked for Butch. He immediately agreed to help her and arrived on her doorstep only minutes later.

"I really appreciate this, Butch," she said with a weary smile.

"No problem. I'm sorry you're having such a hard time. Want me to stay in tomorrow and help?"

She was tempted, but then she shook her head no. "Not yet. Doc will be out tomorrow to lend a hand. If you'll just help him shower and, er, everything and get him in clean clothes, I think he'll sleep a little better."

Tiptoeing upstairs, she opened the door to his room.

"What?" he growled.

"I thought you might enjoy getting cleaned up, Griff. I got Butch to come help out."

Griffin didn't appear pleased, and she remembered his earlier reaction when Butch had called at the house. Should she have asked for another man to help? She was too tired to worry about that now.

"Come on, cowboy," Butch said in hearty tones, stepping around Camille. "Let's go stick you in the shower so the lady won't refuse to have anything to do with you." As he reached for Griff, he nodded toward Camille. "You go do whatever else you have to do, and I'll let you know when we're done."

"I'm going to change the sheets, so I'll be nearby," she assured him. She opened a drawer and pulled out clean underwear and a T-shirt and handed them to Butch.

After the two men disappeared into the bath, she changed the bedding. She was sitting on the side of the bed when the door opened, letting out a little steam along with the two men. "Finished already?" she asked with an extra effort to be cheerful.

"Yeah. Come on, buddy, let's get you back to bed," Butch said.

Griffin said nothing, but Camille read the weariness in his face. Even that short time out of bed had exhausted him.

Once he was tucked into the clean bed, she asked, "Can I get you something to eat?"

"Any ice cream?"

"Sure. I'll be right back."

She motioned for Butch to follow her, and they descended the stairs together. "Thanks for your help."

"Glad to do it. Is he going to be all right?"

"Yes, of course. It's just that chicken pox in men is much more severe."

"Well, call me anytime you need me. And after all this is over and Jake and the guys are back, will you let me take you out to dinner? I'd like to get to know you better."

She smiled, but she also remembered Griff's interpretation of their earlier encounter. She wasn't going to lead anyone on. "That would be nice, but I'm going to be leaving soon."

"Leaving? Where are you going?"

She shrugged. "I think I'm going back to school to get some special training. I have to find a way to support myself now."

"That's a damn shame. But I'll count on at least having dinner with you." He leaned down and kissed her cheek, as she had done to him earlier, so she couldn't complain.

"Good night, Butch."

When she returned to Griff's bedside, he had his eyes closed. As she sat down on the edge of the bed, he opened them, however, and reached for another pillow to shove behind his head. "Where'd that cowboy go?"

"Butch? Do you need him again?"

"I didn't need him at all," he protested with a burr of exhaustion in his voice.

"I thought you would protest if I helped you shower," she countered, and then remembered his earlier behavior when she was trying to awaken him. Maybe he wouldn't have protested after all.

"Did you kiss him again?"

"No!" And she wasn't going to mention that Butch had kissed her.

"Then why are you blushing?"

"Probably because I'm tired," she snapped.

One shaky finger traced her cheek. Then he asked softly, "How are you doing?"

Her heart flipped over. How sweet for him to be

concerned for her. "Fine. How about you?" She couldn't help but reach out and push his hair back from his forehead.

"I feel like an idiot."

"Why? Catching the chicken pox wasn't your idea."

"I should've caught them as a kid, but my mother didn't want me to play much with other children."

"You went to public school?"

"Yeah. But I came home afterward. She worked out of the house. She bought me a computer and encouraged me to entertain myself with it."

He paused, and she slipped a spoonful of ice cream in.

"Don't try to talk too much. Doc said you had to rest."

"You're probably more tired than me."

She gave him another bite of ice cream.

By the time the ice cream was gone, he was almost asleep. He scooted over a little and patted the bed beside him.

"What?" she asked, confused.

"Lie down a few minutes. Keep me company."

She stared at him. "You're kidding, aren't you?"

Almost like Toby, his lips turned down. "I've been lonely."

"You're supposed to rest."

"I'll be resting. Besides, you owe me one. I had to put up with Butch."

She started to protest his words about Butch, but as tired as she was, the bed looked so comfortable.

With a sigh, she slid next to him, resting her head against the pillow. "Okay. Just for a minute."

His arm tightened around her, pulling her a little closer. Then he kissed her brow.

His warmth was probably from fever, but it was soothing to her tired body. She wouldn't stay. But she deserved this moment out of time.

That was her last conscious thought.

Until seven o'clock the next morning when a booming voice awakened her from the doorway.

"What the hell is going on around here?"

Chapter Eleven

Camille struggled to open her eyes. Her ears told her Jake Randall was back home. That couldn't be true.

But it was.

And he was staring at her and Griffin as if they'd committed a mortal sin.

"Calm down, Jake. It's not what you think," Griffin protested, his voice rusty.

"It sure as hell better not be," Jake said, his voice a little calmer.

"Daddy?" Toby called from down the hall.

Camille heard his feet pounding as he sprinted for his father.

"Where's Mom?"

"She's not here yet, son. Pete and I came ahead, but the rest of them are in San Francisco, taking an extra day." After giving Toby a hug, he asked, "Have you been missing school?"

"Not a single day. I tried to stay home because of Torie and Caroline, but Camille and Uncle Griff said I had to go."

Camille had gotten awake enough to start pushing back the covers. She was still dressed in jeans and shirt. She even wore her tennis shoes. She looked up to find Jake staring at her.

"I accidentally fell asleep," she muttered.

"What about Torie and Caroline? Is something wrong?"

"Chicken pox," Toby announced succinctly.

Jake spun around, as if he intended to race off to Caroline's room.

"Wait, Jake. Don't awaken the girls." Camille tucked the cover back around Griffin. "Are you feeling better?" she asked.

"I think my fever's come back," he said with a sigh.

Jake stared at his cousin. "Are you sick, too? What do you have?"

Toby supplied the answer again. "Chicken pox."

Pete appeared behind Jake in the doorway. "The boys are still sleeping. And they have red dots on their faces."

Toby sighed. "Chicken pox," he repeated a second time.

Camille smiled. "Maybe you should wear a sign, Toby, so you won't have to tell them a hundred times." She started for the door. "I need to get Griffin more medicine and something to drink. Then I'll fix you a quick breakfast, Toby. Go get dressed. Maybe your dad will drive you to the bus stop this morning."

"Of course I will. Look, I didn't mean to sound

so—so censorious earlier. I was surprised. But I didn't like the idea of you two— I mean, it might be hard to explain to Toby,'' Jake explained, his cheeks almost as red as Camille's. He immediately changed the subject after she nodded. ''But how long has this been going on, Camille? And where are Red and Mildred? Don't tell me they overslept, too.''

She tried to smooth her hair with her hands as she eased past Pete and Jake. ''No, they're in Cheyenne, where Mildred's cousin lives. The lady fell and broke her hip and didn't have anyone else to take care of her.''

''And Red left you here alone?'' Jake demanded, his voice rising in exasperation.

''No, he left me here with Griff, who has been terrific. At the time, we didn't know we were going to have an outbreak of chicken pox.''

''Couldn't you have called Red to come home?'' Pete asked reasonably, more relaxed than his brother.

''Of course. But Griff just came down with it yesterday, so I hadn't quite decided what to do. Besides, the cleaning ladies have been helping me.''

''How bad do the boys have it?'' Pete asked.

Jake murmured about checking on Caroline, while Camille, with Pete following after her, went down to the kitchen.

''They're doing all right. Better actually now that both of them are sick. Richard couldn't understand why Russell didn't want to play.''

They'd reached the kitchen, and she began preparing breakfast. As soon as she had the bacon cooking, she poured a glass of lemonade and got Griffin's medicine. "Can you take this up to Griff? He'll need help drinking because he doesn't have much strength."

"Sure. Anything else?"

"As soon as the boys wake up, they'll want an oatmeal bath. There's a packet in the bathroom. After they've soaked awhile, gently dry them off and apply lotion to their bumps. Oh, and encourage them not to scratch."

Pete took the glass and medicine and disappeared.

Camille told herself she could've managed, but the relief that filled her that some of the Randalls had returned made her less confident.

As she turned the bacon, Jake entered the kitchen. "The girls are still asleep, except for Miss Torie," he said, carrying the baby. "I changed her diaper and I think she's hungry."

"Yes, I'm sure she is. She was the first with the chicken pox, and she's getting better. Can you fix her a bottle?"

"Sure. We owe you a lot, Camille, for keeping things going, taking such good care of our babies."

She smiled over her shoulder at him as he poured formula into a baby bottle. "You'd better think of a real big treat for Toby, too. He has been wonderful. We couldn't have managed without him."

"You mean something more than a coconut?" Jake asked, a grin on his face.

"How did you know he was concerned about that gift?"

"I teased him before I left. He tried hard to look enthusiastic, but he's not a good actor."

"Maybe not, but he's a terrific family man, just like the other Randalls. Including Griff. Griff cleaned, cooked and took care of the little ones."

"Glad to hear it. He's not used to a lot of family."

She smiled but said nothing else. She wanted to give Griff his due, but she didn't want to initiate any discussions about what Jake saw this morning.

As if he read her mind, he asked, "What was going on this morning?"

Stirring the eggs she was scrambling, she considered her answer. Finally, she said, "I was talking to him, to see how he was doing, and I fell asleep because I was so tired. I must've run up and down those stairs a million times yesterday."

"So he behaved himself?"

She spun around to stare at him. "Jake Randall, how dare you accuse Griff of—of..."

"Now, Cammy, you're Megan's sister, family, you know. I feel responsible. And we all know Griff is, ahem, attracted to you."

Though her cheeks were bright red, she turned back to the eggs before they could burn. "Griff and I understand each other, Jake. And he's a gentleman." Well, most of the time. The kiss when he passed out was a bit of a surprise, but she wasn't going to mention that. Or his hallucinations or dreams or whatever they were.

Pete came back down. "I think Griff is ready for breakfast, Camille."

"Good, thanks, Pete. Jake, you'd better go tell Toby breakfast is ready."

She put the platter of eggs and bacon on the table and began making toast. As soon as Jake returned with Toby, she fixed a plate for Griffin and left the menfolk in charge at the breakfast table.

"Griff? Are you hungry?" she asked as she slipped into his room. His eyes were closed, but they flickered open as soon as she spoke.

"Yeah. I need to get my strength back."

"No, right now you need to rest. You're still running a fever." She crossed to the bed and settled down on the edge of it.

"Did Jake give you a rough time?" he asked as she arranged pillows behind his back.

Her arms were almost around his head, and she looked down at him with a smile. "Yes, and he blamed you."

When Griff frowned, she realized he didn't recognize her teasing. "I'm teasing you, Griff. Everything's fine. I explained that I fell asleep because I was too tired."

"Because I left you stranded."

"Open up." She stuck a bite of eggs in his mouth. "You didn't choose to get sick. You need to remember that."

He sighed. "I know, but it was rotten timing."

"Have a drink of milk."

"Milk? Don't I get coffee?"

"Milk is good for you. Now, eat your breakfast and drink your milk." She spoke as if she were addressing one of the twins.

Griff's eyes narrowed. "Hmm. What bribe do I get?"

"Bribe? You mean you want a cookie afterward?"

"No, not a cookie. If I drink my milk, I think I should get a morning kiss. On the lips," he added firmly.

Camille couldn't help smiling. He sounded so much like one of the little boys. "Okay. One kiss for one glass of milk."

Without another word, he picked up the glass and downed the entire contents. Camille stared at him in amazement.

"Where's my kiss?"

She took the napkin she'd added to his tray and wiped off his milk mustache. Then she leaned forward for a chaste kiss on his sexy lips.

That kind of kiss wasn't what he had in mind. One arm came around her neck, and he pressed her against him, his lips moving against hers, urging her mouth to open to his.

"Ahem! Am I interrupting?" Doc asked from the doorway.

Camille sat up so quickly, she almost tumbled the tray to the floor. "Doc! I didn't know you were stopping by."

"Yeah, I thought I'd better check on Griff here, but he seems to be doing real well."

"He—he was still running a fever this morning. And he wants coffee. Is that all right?" She was afraid Griffin was going to say something inappropriate, so she stuck more eggs in his mouth as he opened it.

"Coffee's fine. Why don't you bring us both up one. I left early so I could come by here. Didn't get my usual cup."

She looked at Griffin and the food left on the plate. "Okay. Do you want to finish feeding him?"

"Be glad to."

She gave Doc the tray and hurried from the room.

Doc settled down in the chair and scooped up a forkful of eggs. "You're getting real good service, Griff."

"Yeah," Griffin agreed, chewing his eggs and avoiding Doc's stare.

"You get any medicine this morning?"

"Yeah." He reached over and picked up a piece of toast from the tray.

"We'll need to take your temperature before you drink that hot coffee. But it looks like you might be having a mild case."

"So I can get up?"

"Absolutely not. You've got at least a couple more days in bed. And maybe longer."

Jake entered the room with two mugs of coffee. "I understand someone wants coffee in here."

Doc took his with a sigh of appreciation. Griffin

discovered he wasn't that anxious for coffee after all. Especially when it was delivered by his eagle-eyed cousin.

"Griff and Camille seem to be getting along just fine," Doc said casually, and Griff almost spilled his coffee.

He set his cup on the lamp table. "Doc," he said warningly.

Jake's expression sharpened. "What do you mean?"

"I interrupted them kissing this morning. And I'm not sure *what* was going on when Griff passed out yesterday." Doc picked up Griffin's second piece of toast and took a bite.

Jake eyed his cousin, and Griff couldn't meet his glance. He knew he had no business kissing Camille, but she was so tempting.

"I'll discuss that with Griff later. Now I need to ask you about Anna," Jake said, his voice turning serious.

"Anna? What's wrong with Anna?" Doc dropped his lazy teasing at once. Anna frequently assisted in his office, in addition to acting as midwife for the county.

"She's expecting again. Will the chicken pox be a problem?"

"Lord have mercy. Yes, it will. Is she here?"

"No. Pete and I came ahead. The others are in San Francisco for a day of shopping."

"Well, it's not like measles, but the more she

avoids illness, the better off she'll be. Can they stay in San Francisco a few days longer?''

Griffin groaned. "I'll pick up the bill for an extended stay, Jake."

Jake stared at him. "You think the chicken pox is your fault, cuz?"

"Well, I—"

"Don't be foolish, boy," Doc admonished. "Though it's a nice offer. Brett can pay for his own second honeymoon. You should concentrate on your first."

Griffin stared at him, his mouth open, and Jake laughed. "You sure shut him up, Doc. I'll go call San Francisco, then take Toby to the bus stop. See you later."

As soon as Jake had left the room, Griff grabbed Doc's arm. "Doc, what you saw was— I mean, I'm not getting married. Ever."

Doc sipped his coffee, then said, "You sure are a Randall. Are all of you born with fear of marriage, or are you taught it from the cradle?"

"I was taught from the cradle…by my mother." Griff sank back against the pillows, suddenly tired.

"You'd best rest, boy. Remember, stay in bed. And if you don't want to get burned, you shouldn't play with matches." Without waiting for an answer, he left the room, coffee mug in hand.

Griff finished his piece of toast and sipped his coffee, thinking about what Doc had said. He was right, damn it. Griff had no business kissing Camille so much. So why was he doing it, other than because of Camille's sexiness?

Was he changing his mind? Had his cousins' happy marriages made him believe in everlasting love? Confusion filled him. He didn't know what to think.

After another sip of his coffee, he gave in to the exhaustion filling him and drifted off to sleep, thoughts of Camille on his mind.

WITH PETE AND JAKE HOME, everything seemed easier and in no time things returned to normal.

Which brought something else to Camille's mind.

"Jake, did Doc say anything to you about Griff's father?"

Jake, holding Caroline and Elizabeth on his knees, jerked his head up. "What about Griff's father?"

"He seemed to think he knew who Griff's father is," Camille said, frowning. "I told him to wait until you got back. I'm not sure Griff wants to know."

"I'm not sure he does, either. But I think he'll have to face it sooner or later if he stays around."

Camille's heart lurched. "Do you think he's going to stay around?"

"I don't know. But he's stayed so far," Jake said, smoothing back Caroline's bangs and teasing first one and then the other little girl. "These two sure are sweethearts."

Camille wasn't distracted. "Has he said anything about staying? He told me he's returning to Chicago."

"I hope not. But life here is a big change for him. I'm glad he managed so well while we were gone. Did he work with Butch at all?"

"The first few days he rode with the cowboys every day. When he returned to the house, it was always after dinner and he seemed tired. Afterward, when Red and Mildred left, he stayed here with me but talked to Butch on the phone. And Butch came to the house and offered to help because they were caught up."

"Hmm, I wouldn't give Butch much credit for offering. He was probably hoping to flirt with you."

Camille rolled her eyes. "That's what Griff said, too. You'd think I was a siren or something."

Jake grinned. "Griff and I understand men, and believe me, you're plenty of temptation."

Camille blushed and tried to change the subject. "Did you speak to Brett and Anna? Are they going to stay in San Francisco a few days?"

"Yeah, once I convinced them Torie was okay. They'll be calling again this evening."

"And the rest of them will be home tomorrow?"

"Yeah. B.J. and Janie were going to get on a plane at once, but I convinced them to have their day of shopping. The girls don't get to do much shopping in the general run of things."

"But they seem content."

"Yeah, but—"

Knocking on the back door interrupted them.

"I'll get it," Camille said, since Jake had his arms full of girls.

A man about Red's age or a little older stood on the back porch.

"Hello?"

"Is Jake Randall here?"

"Yes, he is. Come in."

The man followed her into the kitchen.

"I'll take the girls, Jake. This man is here to see you."

"Morning, Haney," Jake said as he stood. "Is there any more coffee, Camille?"

"Yes, the pot's on the stove. Girls, let's go see what Uncle Pete and the twins are doing." She left with a last glance over her shoulder. Bill Haney owned the ranch nearby that Jake was talking about buying.

"HAVE A SEAT. I'll pour us some coffee," Jake suggested, smiling at the older man.

"Appreciate it," he said and settled in at the table.

Jake set a mug of coffee in front of him and joined him at the table. When Haney said nothing, he asked, "What brings you by?"

"Heard Margaret's boy is here."

"Yeah. Margaret died recently and asked to be buried on the ranch. Griff brought her body home."

"Griff? That's his name?"

"Griffin. Griffin Randall."

Haney stared at his coffee, and Jake waited.

"Where is he? Is he still here?"

"Yeah. He's upstairs in bed. Got the chicken pox."

Haney grunted.

"Have you thought about the offer we made for your place?" Jake finally asked. "I think it was a fair offer."

"I've thought about it."

More silence.

"Well?" Jake prodded.

"Still thinking. It depends on things."

Jake took a sip of his coffee. He couldn't do much to rush the old man. And he had a suspicion of the problem.

Pete strolled into the kitchen.

"Hello. Didn't know we had company. How are you, Mr. Haney?" He stuck out his hand and shook their guest's. Then he said, "You here about the offer we made?"

"Sort of."

"Sit down and join us, Pete," Jake said.

Something in Jake's voice must've shown his tension to his brother. Pete, after a quick look at his brother, sat down at the table.

"You know," he said, smiling, "we're interested in the land, but arrangements could be made for you to stay in the house as long as you want."

Haney grunted again. Then he asked, "Why do you need more land?"

"We want our cousin to stay here, and he deserves his own place, though he hasn't asked for anything," Jake explained.

"What's he like?"

Pete looked confused, but Jake watched his neighbor as he said, "Everyone says he looks a lot like me."

Haney grunted again.

Pete leaned forward, frowning. "You haven't met him?" Then he nodded to himself. "That's right. You didn't come to Margaret's burial."

"No."

"Well, Griff's a great guy. He was a successful stockbroker in Chicago. But we're hoping he'll stay here."

Haney nodded in Pete's direction but turned his gaze to Jake. "Does he know?"

Jake shook his head no.

Pete looked even more confused. "Are you talking about me?"

"No. The boy."

"The boy?"

Haney said slowly, "I mean Griffin."

"Does he know what?" Pete demanded, apparently becoming fed up with the secrecy.

Haney looked first at Pete and then Jake. Finally, he answered, "That I'm his father."

Chapter Twelve

Pete stared at the old man. Then he looked at his brother. "How did you know?"

"I didn't, for sure. I just suspected. Things Dad said, his feelings about Haney. I remember Dad visiting him once."

"He came to ask me if I'd heard from Margaret. I knew then that he knew. I was ashamed. I figured you all knew." Haney kept his gaze fixed on the table.

"My brothers weren't even aware of Margaret's existence," Jake said softly.

"Is that why you kept to yourself all these years?" Pete asked.

Haney nodded.

Jake abruptly stood and crossed the kitchen to re-fill his coffee mug. "Look, Haney, we all do things we shouldn't. I'm not standing in judgment of your actions." He took a sip of coffee and leaned against the cabinet. "But I won't lie to you. The man who has a beef with you is upstairs."

Haney nodded again.

"What do you want us to do?"

"I don't know." The older man rubbed his face, weariness showing there and in his sagging shoulders.

"I can tell him…when he's well," Jake said. "But he'll have more respect for you if you do it."

Haney nodded again. "Call me when he's recovered."

Then Bill Haney got up and walked out of the house without another word.

Jake stared after him, a considering look on his face.

"What do you think he's going to do?" Pete asked.

"About Griff?"

"No, about selling us the ranch. What do you think will happen?" Pete insisted.

"That all depends on Griff."

MUCH TO JAKE'S SURPRISE, his wife, Janie, Megan and Chad returned that afternoon. When they discovered that even Griff was down with the chicken pox, B.J. chastised Jake for not telling them how difficult things had been on the ranch.

But everything really was back to normal the next morning. With B.J. taking the rest of the week off, Janie still considering herself on vacation and Megan not opening the store, suddenly the house seemed full again.

Leaving Camille to concentrate on *her* patient.

First thing after showering and dressing, she scooted down the hall to the bedroom Griff was using.

She slipped into his room, and his eyes fluttered open.

"How are you this morning?"

"Still feeling pretty low," he muttered, "but you make things better."

"Aren't you glad we're not on our own anymore?" she asked with a smile.

"I don't know. I hated letting you down, but I kind of miss our being alone."

Her heartbeat sped up. "Alone with six kids."

"Yeah, but they were good kids. How are they doing?"

"Torie is almost well. Doc said she had a light case. The girls are doing better. And the twins are in the middle of it. Once you break out, you'll feel better, too."

"Ah. Something to look forward to." He closed his eyes, and she debated whether she should leave him alone.

"Are you going to give me baths when I break out?" he asked, reaching out to catch her hand before she could move away.

"Of course not!" she protested, her cheeks red. "Jake or one of the other Randalls will help you."

"Hmm. Got any milk you want me to drink this morning?"

She blinked at his change of subject. "You want milk?"

"No, honey, I just want to be bribed."

"Griff!"

He opened his eyes. "Sorry. I got a little lonely yesterday when everyone arrived home."

"I thought they all came in to see you," she said softly, moving to sit on the edge of his bed.

"Yeah, but I didn't see you."

Camille told herself he was toying with her, but she couldn't keep her heart from melting. "I thought maybe you were tired of me."

Before answering, he struggled to slide a couple of pillows behind his head, raising him higher. "If I promise to drink the milk when you bring it, can I have my bribe now?"

She didn't bother answering with words. Instead, she leaned forward, letting her lips cover his, tasting the excitement that his touch brought. She was aware of his fever, but she'd bring him medicine later.

No one interrupted their embrace. But wisdom finally prevailed over attraction, and Camille pulled back.

Griffin fell back on the pillows with a sigh. "Let's try that again when I'm back at full strength."

"I don't think I'll dare. We might forget that neither of us is interested in—in a future together," she replied, her breathing returning to normal.

Griffin frowned, staring at her. "Yeah."

"I'll go downstairs and get you some medicine and something to drink." She left the room, afraid if she stayed any longer, she'd lose whatever good sense she had.

Janie and Pete were at the breakfast table, mugs of coffee in front of them. "Morning, Camille."

"Hi. How are the kids this morning?"

"Still sleeping," Pete said with a grin. "As soon as they wake up, we'll get started on the oatmeal baths."

Janie shook her head. "I don't know how you managed all these patients, Camille. It makes me tired just thinking about it."

"You got fat and lazy in Hawaii," Pete teased.

The slamming of a door upstairs stopped Janie from responding. All three stared at each other, wondering if they should investigate. Before they could do so, however, Jake burst into the kitchen, his face angry.

"Something the matter, brother?" Pete asked.

"Yeah, women!"

Camille felt her mouth drop open. Jake was complaining about women? He always cautioned his brothers to consider their wives.

Pete and Janie seemed as stunned as Camille. As Jake poured himself a cup of coffee, Pete cleared his throat. "Uh, Jake, you and B.J. have an argument?"

Jake sent an angry look his brother's way and walked out the back door.

"Wow, that was—" Janie began.

She halted because angry steps could be heard on the stairs. Then B.J. swept into the kitchen. While she hid her emotions a little more than Jake, it was clear she was upset.

"Are there any biscuits?"

Janie jumped up. "Sure. I put them back in the oven so they'd stay warm." She took them out. "Want a plate?"

"No. I'm going on an emergency call. Just wrap one in a napkin." She searched the cabinets until she found a foam cup that she filled with coffee.

"Don't you want to sit down and eat a proper meal?" Janie asked.

"No. My patients are important," B.J. snapped. Then she stopped and closed her eyes. When she opened them, she offered an apology to Janie. "Sorry, I didn't mean to snap at you."

"That's okay. How's Caroline this morning?"

"Still asleep. Megan promised to bathe her with Elizabeth this morning. Sorry I won't be here to give you a break, Camille."

"No problem. There's a lot of help around." Camille smiled, but it was a guarded smile. She wasn't sure what was going on.

With a brief goodbye, B.J. left the house.

"What do you think that was about?" Pete asked. "Is it because she's taking a call when she's supposed to be on vacation?"

"I don't know," Janie said, "but I've never seen Jake mad at B.J."

All Camille could think about was what Griffin had predicted. "I need to take Griff his medicine and something to drink."

"What about breakfast for him? I can scramble some eggs, if you want," Janie offered.

"That would be nice. And after breakfast, Pete, could you help him take a shower?"

"Sure. Be glad to."

She escaped back up the stairs with another glass of lemonade and medicine.

And discovered that Griffin didn't have to be told about the latest development.

He was lying there with his eyes open when she walked in.

"Hi. I brought you some breakfast," she said brightly, a smile on her lips.

"What happened?"

"What are you talking about?" she asked, hoping he wasn't talking about Jake and B.J.

"I'm talking about the fight that occurred across the hall this morning," he said firmly.

"Fight? We didn't hear a fight."

"Jake and B.J. were yelling at each other."

Camille tried to dismiss his statement. "Married couples can't always agree, Griff. I'm sure it was nothing."

HE FELT TRAPPED.

Griffin had to stay down. Not only Doc, but also Camille would be on his back if he didn't follow orders. But he hated staying in bed. And he hated feeling so weak. And he hated thinking he'd brought unhappiness to his cousins.

Pete helped him into the shower. It was embarrassing how weak he felt. He could only stand for a few minutes. But getting cleaned up made him feel better. When he came out of the bathroom, in a fresh T-shirt and briefs, the two men found Camille finishing up changing the linens on his bed. She ignored his embarrassment and pulled back the covers.

"Come on, Griff, right back in bed. You've had a busy morning and you need to sleep until lunch."

"That's all I do is sleep," he grumbled, his gaze raking her curves. Suddenly, he was hungry for her touch, for those kisses that he couldn't forget, for what he couldn't have.

Pete helped lower him to the mattress. Then Camille tucked the covers around him. "Do you need anything else?"

He caught Pete's grin and ignored it. "No, nothing."

Camille brushed his still-damp hair off his forehead. "Then get some sleep."

"Yeah," he muttered. "Uh, when Jake comes for lunch, could you ask him to come see me?"

Pete and Camille exchanged a look. Then Pete spoke. "Jake's not in a very good mood right now, Griff. Maybe I could help you?"

"No. I need to see Jake."

"Okay. We'll pass on the message."

They left the room, leaving Griffin alone. And that was something he was going to have to get used to all over again. 'Cause he'd rather leave and be alone than ruin what his cousins had going here.

JAKE CAME IN FOR LUNCH, but B.J. hadn't returned home. Pete, Janie and Camille had discussed the early-morning brouhaha with Megan and Chad, and they all watched Jake as if he were a lion with a wounded paw.

He still appeared to be in a foul mood. Finally, Pete said, "Uh, Jake, Griff asked if you'd stop by his room after you eat. Seems he needs to talk to you about something."

"Okay," Jake muttered.

"Is something wrong?" Megan asked. "Isn't he feeling better?"

"Yes," Camille said hesitantly. "I think something happened this morning to upset him."

Several pairs of eyes gazed in Jake's direction.

"What was it?" Megan innocently asked.

Jake stood up and threw down his napkin. "Damn it, everyone needs to mind his own business!"

The entire table seemed shocked by Jake's words. It appeared he was disgruntled with a lot of things this morning. Finally, he said, "I apologize. It's been a difficult morning. But I shouldn't take it out on you. Now, what does Griff want to talk to me about?"

Pete shrugged his shoulders. "He didn't say."

"Camille?"

Reluctantly, she said, "I think he overheard you and B.J. this morning. He seemed disturbed. But, Jake, he doesn't have much energy. He shouldn't be upset."

"Yes, Mother Hen. I'll be careful. Should I take some lunch up to him?"

"I was going to feed him as soon as we finish. He's still asleep right now, as far as I know."

"Okay, after you feed him, I'll stop by and have a chat. About something," Jake said to Camille, his voice rough.

She nodded in agreement and hurriedly finished her lunch. Then she filled a plate for Griffin and, with a secret smile, added a glass of milk to the tray.

When she reached Griffin's room, she entered to discover Griffin still asleep. She set the tray on the lamp table by the bed and touched Griffin's shoulder.

"Griff? Are you ready for lunch?"

Slowly, his eyes opened, and he gave Camille such a sweet smile she almost wished she could join him in the bed. "I've brought your lunch."

Shaking himself completely awake, he ignored the food. "Where's Jake?"

"He said he'd stop by for a chat after you eat lunch."

"I need to talk to Jake."

"You need to keep your strength up. *Then* you can talk to Jake." She figured she had a career as an army sergeant when she left the ranch.

"Is B.J. here?" he asked after taking his first bite.

"No, she went out on a call."

"It's like I said, Cammy. But I didn't mean it," he said, his voice anguished.

"What are you talking about?" Camille asked, hoping she was wrong in what she suspected.

"I'm talking about B.J. and Jake's argument. It's my fault."

"Don't be silly. Married couples argue. It couldn't be your fault."

He dismissed her words. "I couldn't overhear everything, but they were discussing the size of the family. And my name came up several times. I think my staying here has put a strain on everyone. I knew I shouldn't have. I'm leaving as soon as I get mobile again."

"Griff, that's ridiculous. Your being here has been a help, not a complication. You must've misunderstood." She certainly hoped he had. "If that were true, then they wouldn't want me here, either. And they've been completely welcoming."

"Look, Camille, you've got stars in your eyes about life here. It's not a fairy tale. People aren't always happy. And I'm right about married couples. Sometimes it just doesn't last. But I'm not going to do anything to ruin Jake's marriage if I can help it. And I can."

"This doesn't make sense, Griff!" she argued.

"A lot of things don't make sense. But B.J. must be fed up with me hanging around, and Jake's refusing to throw me out. Just because you want to believe everything will always be happy doesn't make it that way. You've got to face reality some time!"

Camille resented the scorn in his voice. He thought she was a Pollyanna, only seeing the good in everyone? Maybe she was once, but not after her fiancé absconded with her money.

She knew better than to believe in everyone.

But the Randalls...? She could believe in the Randalls for her entire life, and she knew she'd be right.

"Believe what you want, Griffin Randall. You're wrong, though. B.J. doesn't mind if you stay, and you're not the cause of their argument. And furthermore, they won't break up. B.J. and Jake Randall will be happy and married long after you've gone, and don't you forget it!"

She stomped from the room and slammed the door behind her.

CAMILLE WAS CLEANING UP after lunch when Jake came back downstairs. She said nothing, but she couldn't help looking at his expression, hoping to discover what had happened in Griff's bedroom.

"Camille, did you talk to Griff?" Jake asked, coming to a stop beside her at the sink.

"Um, yes." She didn't know how much to admit.

"He's got some damn fool notion that he's not welcome here anymore." Jake rubbed the back of his neck. "Did anyone say anything to him to make him think that?"

"He didn't explain?"

Jake shook his head no. "Explain what?"

Camille almost groaned aloud. Great. Now she had to explain. "He heard you and B.J. arguing this morning," she said, keeping her gaze on the glass she was rinsing. "He thought he heard his name mentioned, along with—with something about a bigger family."

Finally, she looked at Jake's red face. "He thought he'd worn out his welcome."

"Damn!" Jake muttered, his hands on his hips.

Camille frowned at him. "It's not true, is it?"

"That he's worn out his welcome? Of course not. But I couldn't convince him a few minutes ago. Of course, I didn't know then why he thought he should go."

"Can you get B.J. to tell him she wasn't talking about him? That she doesn't mind him staying?" Camille asked.

If anything, Jake's face got redder. "Uh, I don't know. I'm not sure we're talking to each other right now." He sighed. "Don't worry. We've got some time before he'll be strong enough to leave. He was pretty worn-out by the time I got up there."

Guilt filled Camille. "Oh. Um, had he eaten his lunch?"

"No, not much. I thought you were going to feed him."

"I'll go check on him," she said, hoping to end the conversation before Jake asked any more questions. She wiped her hands and headed for the stairs.

"You tell him he's not going anywhere, you hear?" Jake called behind her.

Camille wished she believed that.

EVERYONE SURREPTITIOUSLY watched Jake and B.J. at dinner that evening. Though B.J. usually sat on

Jake's right, tonight Toby took that place, with his mother next to him.

"Back at work already, B.J.?" Chad asked, before Megan elbowed him in his ribs.

"Yes." B.J. didn't offer any explanation.

"How's Griff doing?" Pete asked, and everyone but Camille relaxed.

"He's weak."

"We're going to have to think of a way to thank him for helping with the kids," Megan said. "After all, he wouldn't be sick if he hadn't stayed and helped out."

Everyone nodded in agreement.

Megan wasn't finished. "I really hate for him to leave. He fits in so well here."

Camille immediately looked at B.J., but she said nothing.

Jake leaned back in his chair. "I'm hoping to convince him to stay. He's changed a lot since that first day. I think he'll be happy here."

Chewing on her bottom lip, Camille debated what to say. Finally, she took a chance. "He doesn't think everyone feels that way."

Chapter Thirteen

Those words got everyone's attention. "What are you talking about?" Pete demanded.

Several others asked the same thing.

Camille stared at Jake and B.J.

Jake shook his head. "You shouldn't have said anything, Camille. I said I'd work it out."

There was another uproar of questions, and Jake held up his hand. "Look, it's a misunderstanding, that's all."

To Camille's surprise, it was B.J. who pressed for an explanation. "I think you should tell us what Camille is talking about."

Jake glared at his wife and said nothing.

Camille jumped in. "He's talking about your argument this morning. Griff overheard some of it, and he got the impression he'd outstayed his welcome."

B.J. stared at Camille and then turned her anger to her husband. "And you let him think that? That *I* didn't want him here?"

Jake, without regard to his audience, fired back.

"Well, I sure as hell wasn't going to have a heart-to-heart with him about our problems."

Deathly silence centered on the table.

Then Pete, with a casual, offhand approach that fooled no one, said, "You guys having problems?"

"I'm not discussing it with you, either," Jake assured everyone.

"I don't see why not. According to you, it affects all of them, too," B.J. said coolly.

"B.J.," Jake said, a warning in his voice.

His wife, however, was no wimp, and would not back off because her husband was upset. She looked at the other women at the table. "The problem is I want to have another baby, like Anna."

Shock ran through the group. Jake, family-man Jake, the man who'd always promoted the idea of family, didn't want to have another child?

Camille leaned forward, wanting to be sure she was correct in her assessment. "You don't want another child, Jake?"

Toby answered before Jake could. "I do! I want a brother."

Jake ignored him. "This is a personal argument. It has nothing to do with the rest of you."

"Yes, it does. You told me it would put too much work on everyone," B.J. retorted. "You said I was asking everyone else to raise my children."

After a shocked silence, there was a jumble of responses, most from the women, assuring B.J. that was not true.

It was Toby, however, who quietened everyone.

With a panicky look on his little face, he tugged on Jake's sleeve. "Are you and Mom angry with each other? Are you going to get a divorce?"

"A divorce? What made you think that?" Jake demanded, his brows furrowed.

"One of my friends at school, Eric, his parents argued, and then his daddy left." Toby's bottom lip trembled. "I told him it couldn't happen to us 'cause you loved each other."

B.J. bowed her head. Camille suspected it was to hide the sudden tears that filled her eyes.

Jake leaned over and hugged Toby. "You're exactly right, Toby. Your mom and I aren't going to get a divorce."

"Then why are you arguing?"

Jake looked from Toby down the length of the table, at all the waiting faces. With a sigh, he clasped his hands over his plate and said, "Look, I shouldn't have to discuss this in front of all of you, but—but it's not that I don't want another child. It's that I want B.J. healthy and happy. And she's working ten or twelve hours a day. She doesn't have time for another child, much less the energy and stamina another pregnancy would require. She's not that young, you know."

"Man, no wonder you had an argument," Pete said with a whistle. "Even I know better than to tell a woman she's getting old."

Chad chuckled, but no one else even smiled.

"Jake's not going to give up his work for us to have another child," B.J. explained. "I don't think it's fair that he asks me to do so. I worked hard and long to become a vet.''

"I'm willing to cut back my hours to help take care of the kids,'' Jake returned. "But I can't be the one pregnant. And you know when the baby is little, you're going to worry about him or her. I can't stop that, either.''

B.J. fired back, and several of the ladies added argument, but it was Chad who halted the battle. "I have an idea,'' he said loudly. Then he said it again. Gradually, silence fell.

"Nothing you can say—'' Jake began.

"Wait and see. I was visiting with Glen Davis on the other side of the county in Rawhide yesterday.''

Before he could continue, Jake interrupted. "I don't care who you talked to. This problem is about B.J. and me.''

Chad continued as if Jake hadn't spoken. "His son is finishing veterinarian school in January.''

Now he had everyone's attention.

"Glen wants his son close to home, but he figured B.J. had this area covered, and he wouldn't want his son in competition with a good friend.'' Chad smiled at B.J. "Why not offer the guy a partnership and cut back on your hours? By the time you have the baby and are ready to go back to work, there should be enough business for the two of you.''

Camille held her breath, waiting for the couple's response.

Their gazes met over Toby's anxious face. Then

Jake abruptly stood. "B.J. and I are going to go upstairs to talk."

He took her arm as she stood, and they headed for the door. Just before he left the room, he looked back over his shoulder. "Thanks, little brother. I owe you one."

GRIFF HEARD the slight tap on his door and both hoped and feared it was Camille returning to feed him dinner. He felt very unsettled, what with his concern about being on the ranch and his mixed feelings about Camille. "Come in."

When Jake appeared, Griff let out a sigh. "Hi, Jake."

"How's everything going?" he asked, a cheerful smile on his face.

Griff narrowed his gaze. That smile was certainly a difference from Jake's demeanor earlier that day. "What's up?"

"Nothing," Jake said.

"Why are you smiling? Earlier today you wouldn't even look me in the eye, much less act happy."

"I didn't want to tell you earlier, but B.J. and I were having a little problem."

"Come on, Jake, everyone in the house knew that. That's why I told you I had to leave. I'm not going to be the one to break up the happy home."

"Yeah, but you didn't tell me that today. You said you needed to go back to Chicago. You said you were homesick. You said a lot of things that weren't true."

"So did you," Griff countered.

Jake gave an embarrassed chuckle and rubbed the back of his neck. "Yeah, I guess I did." Then he looked Griff in the eye. "But I'm not lying now. B.J. and I cleared up our little problem, and it had nothing to do with you."

"Then why did I hear my name mentioned several times?"

"Because B.J. wants to have another baby. She pointed out several times that your being here hadn't caused a problem. She didn't see why another baby would, either."

Griff blinked several times. "Well, as an adult, I can generally take care of myself," he declared.

"I know. But we've worked out our problem. She's going to take on a partner and cut back her hours."

"Good decision," Griff agreed.

"Yeah," Jake said, a silly grin on his face as he stared across the room.

"I'm not going to ask what you're thinking about," Griff said with a smile. "I think it might be X-rated."

"Yeah," Jake repeated, his smile broadening.

"I'm glad you worked everything out."

"Now all we have to worry about is you."

Griff frowned. "What is there to worry about?"

"You leaving. We want you to stay, Griff."

Griffin looked away. He didn't want his cousin to

see how much those words meant to him. He didn't want them to mean anything. But they did. "I'm not sure that's a good idea," he said slowly.

"Why? You don't need the money. And you could probably do a lot from anywhere with a computer."

Griffin said nothing. He'd already had this discussion with Camille.

"Right?" Jake insisted.

"Yeah. But it's not a good idea. I'm not a family man, like you."

"Of course not, because you had no family. But now you do. And you might even be tempted to make your own family," Jake suggested, a twinkle in his eye. "I think maybe you and Camille got close while we were gone."

"Too close. Lust isn't love, and you know it."

"It's part of love. But you're right, there has to be more."

"So that's why I need to leave." Because, against his better judgment, it was becoming easier and easier to think Jake might be right. After a pause, he added, "Jake, I want to help her."

"Who?" Jake asked, his eyes rounded in innocence.

"Come on, Jake, you know I mean Camille. I think I can help track down her ex-fiancé, maybe even recover some of her money."

"Why do you think you can, if the FBI can't?"

"Because I know stockbrokers. And I care more than the FBI does. But I'm going to need some information from Camille and I don't think she'll tell me anything.''

"Not likely. She hasn't even told Megan all that much.''

Griffin grimaced. "That will make it difficult.''

"Yeah. But maybe if you tell me what you need to know, I can get the answers out of her.''

"Okay. But you'll need to write the questions down.''

Jake fetched a pen and paper, and Griffin dictated the questions he'd need to ask Camille.

He was going to pay Camille back for her concern, her care, by tracking down the bastard who'd stolen her inheritance from her.

Then they'd be square.

And he'd be alone.

And miserable.

CAMILLE WAS RELIEVED that no one commented on her sudden avoidance of the sickroom. After their argument, Griffin had been stiff and formal. She'd decided he didn't want her around anymore. Fortunately, the Randalls went out of their way to ensure she didn't have to face Griffin.

To the point that it was driving her crazy.

So she occupied her time with the babies. Since B.J. had gone back to her animal patients and Janie and Megan to their regular pursuits, she at least felt needed by someone. Even if it wasn't Griffin.

Red and Mildred had called. They'd decided the only possible solution to her cousin's problem was to move her into a nursing home. They were making arrangements and would be back home in a couple of days.

According to Doc, Griffin would be up and around soon, also. Not that she cared, she reminded herself. She had to work hard, however, to keep her mind off of him.

"Say, Camille," Jake greeted her as he entered the kitchen while she was feeding Torie her baby food for breakfast.

"Yes, Jake?" she asked as she scooped the food that didn't go in off Torie's chin and tried again.

"An FBI guy called earlier and needed some more information about your ex-fiancé. I told him I'd get the information and let him know."

Camille hated even to think about Clay and his actions, but she shrugged, knowing she had to give them the information. "Just give me the number and I'll call him. There's no need to take up your time."

"No problem. I've already got the questions here. We can just run through them."

Somehow his response didn't make a lot of sense, but she shrugged. Whatever Jake wanted. He always took care of everyone. It probably made him feel he was doing something for her. She gave him the answers he sought.

"Great!" Jake said, his enthusiasm a lot stronger than hers. "I'll get these to him right away."

"Jake, won't he want to talk to me?" she asked curiously.

"Um, well, he probably will in a few days, but

he's real busy right now,'' Jake said, getting up from the table. ''I'm—I'm going to fax these to him, so it'll be faster.''

''Oh. Okay. But I'm not sure about some of those questions. I already told them who Clay's friends were. They talked to that broker in Chicago.''

''They're just double-checking. You know how precise the FBI can be about every little detail. Probably want to be sure you haven't thought of anything else they need to know.''

''Okay. Tell them I'll answer any other questions they have.'' Though she didn't believe it would make a difference. Clay had probably left the country with her money.

Jake hurried from the kitchen. Camille heard him going up the stairs and wondered why he hadn't gone into the office instead. Surely he didn't have a fax machine in his bedroom?

Torie squealed, indicating Camille had been distracted too long, and she offered another bite of strained peaches to the baby.

At least Torie didn't reject her after every bite.

GRIFF WAS GETTING stronger, but he still had to pace himself. Jake had brought him his laptop computer, and he'd begun the process of looking for the scum who had stolen from Camille.

He'd gotten lucky because he knew the supervisor of Clay's Chicago friend, even though he didn't work at Griffin's old firm. It seemed to Griffin that a man who'd trained as a stockbroker would likely invest in the stock market. After all, that was his area of expertise.

If he did, and couldn't handle the account himself, he'd use a friend, even if he had to lie to him. With that much money involved, maybe the supervisor would be able to check out a few things.

Within a couple of days, he'd uncovered the accounts that Clay had opened with his friend, alerted the FBI and had the accounts frozen. Not all of her money was in those accounts, but a half million had been saved. With luck, they might find more.

Doc visited him just after he received a call from his friend in Chicago.

"You seem wide-awake this morning," Doc said as he entered, Jake right behind him.

"Yeah. Good news, Jake. They've frozen the accounts. Camille will get back some of her money."

"What's this?" Doc asked.

"Terrific! Want me to call her up here so you can tell her?" Jake asked, then added a quick explanation to Doc.

"No. I think we'd better let the FBI tell her. I'm sure they'll contact her soon." Griffin looked away from Jake's piercing gaze. "When can I get up, Doc? I've been in this bed forever."

Doc took out his stethoscope and listened to his heart and lungs, checked his eyes and ears, felt around on him and then set back. "Hmm, I think you might get up for lunch today. Eat at the table with the adults," he teased. "But I want you back in bed for the afternoon. You'll have to build up your strength slowly."

"Take another nap?" Griffin protested with a groan.

"I think you'll be glad to do so. You don't realize how weak you still are."

In truth, he did. Griffin had been irritated at how little he could do before he had to rest. Phone calls and computer work shouldn't exhaust a grown man, but it had.

At least it had been for a good cause.

"Glad to hear about Camille's good fortune," Doc added as he put away his medical tools. "She's a sweet little thing, and pretty as a picture."

Griffin ground his teeth together, fighting the urge to tell Doc he was too old to be thinking about Camille like that.

"Yeah, she's a sweetheart," Jake agreed, grinning at Griff as if he could read his mind.

"Well, I'll be on my way to patients who really need me," Doc said, clapping Griffin on the shoulder. "You take it slow now, and come see me in a couple of days. I can't waste all my time making house calls on you, boy." With a grin, he eased himself out of the chair, shook Jake's hand and left.

Jake stayed.

"Why don't you want to tell Camille about what you've done for her?"

"Because she doesn't want to talk to me."

"She'll be grateful for what you've done."

"I don't need her gratitude. I was just trying to

pay her back for all the care she's given me." He stared at the ceiling, wishing Jake would go away.

"Things would go easier on you, Griff, if you'd just accept your future."

He heard the teasing in Jake's voice, but he couldn't resist asking what he meant. "I don't understand what you're saying."

"I'm saying that little lady has you wrapped around her finger, and you're going to be waltzing down the aisle in the end. You might as well quit resisting and enjoy."

Griffin whipped his head around so he could see Jake. "I told you I'm not going to marry, Jake. I haven't changed my mind."

With a sigh, Jake stood. "Okay, do it your way. I'll see you at lunch."

Three hours later, Jake appeared in the doorway again. "Well, you still want to come down for lunch?"

"Yeah. Any word from the FBI?"

"Not yet."

Griffin frowned even as he shoved back the covers and reached for a pair of sweatpants to wear downstairs. "They should've called already. I wonder what's holding them up."

"They've probably been busy. They have more to do than just lie around, like you." Jake grinned at his cousin.

Griffin chose to ignore his cousin's words. "Am I too informal for lunch?"

"Naw, we only require tuxes for dinner. Come

on, Red and Mildred got back an hour ago, so this will be their welcome-home luncheon, as well as your return. And Brett and Anna will get home this evening. Pete's going to pick them up as soon as we've eaten.''

Griffin leaned on Jake as he descended the stairs, his legs shaky. But when they reached the kitchen door, he straightened his shoulders and walked in alone.

His gaze immediately searched for Camille. He told himself he was only wanting to see her because she'd been an infrequent visitor to his room, unlike the rest of the household. But it was more than that. He was starving for the sight of her.

Red and Mildred greeted him as he rounded the table and he managed to respond, but his gaze never left Camille. She was seated in her regular spot, but he suspected she'd put up a fight about that.

Sliding in beside her, he murmured a hello, but she ignored him. He opened his mouth to greet her again, when the phone rang.

Red answered it and then called Camille to the phone.

''Who was it?'' Jake asked quietly.

''The FBI,'' Red said just as quietly. They all sat silently, watching her.

When her knees buckled under her, Chad was the closest to her and kept her from hitting the floor. Griff wished he'd been in shape so he could've rescued her, but he wasn't sure he could even stand.

"What's wrong?" Megan demanded, just behind Chad.

Camille gave her a trembly smile and picked up the phone again. Then, after a few words, she hung up the phone.

"They've found over a half million of my money," she announced. "The accounts are frozen, and eventually I'll get it back."

"How'd they do that?" Red demanded.

"He didn't explain how they found them. But the stupid man invested in the stock market again, trying to make more money. I can't believe he was so dumb." She returned to her seat at the table.

"Why aren't you jumping for joy?" Megan asked.

"I think it's hard to take it all in."

Before anyone asked more questions, they heard sirens in the distance.

Jake frowned. "Sheriff must have something real important going on. He doesn't use those sirens very often."

"Maybe he's chasing some cattle rustlers," Chad suggested, grinning.

"Maybe," Jake agreed. "Well," he said as everyone got seated, "we've got a lot to be thankful for. So let's give thanks."

Everyone bowed his or her head. Jake led a brief prayer and closed it with a hearty "Amen," echoed around the table.

But the siren, in the meantime, had gotten louder.

Red left the table and crossed to the window over the sink, then turned around.

"I don't know what you've been up to while Mildred and me was gone, but the sheriff ain't chasing no rustlers. He's come down the drive with his lights flashing. Whatever, or whoever, he's after is right here on the Randall ranch."

Chapter Fourteen

All the men headed for the back porch. Mildred and Janie went to the window while Megan exchanged a worried look with Camille.

"What could it be?" Megan asked.

Janie turned from the window. "I don't know, but the sheriff has a stranger in the back seat. I wonder if he's handcuffed."

Megan and Camille came to the window together.

"I don't know him, either," Megan said.

"I do."

The other women turned to stare at Camille. Mildred asked the question they all wanted the answer to. "Who is he?"

"My ex-fiancé." She turned and walked to the door. Whatever the reason Clay had arrived on the ranch, it had to do with her, not the Randalls.

She stepped down off the porch as the sheriff opened the back door of the squad car and assisted Clay Nettles out. He lifted his head and caught sight of her.

"Camille!" he called, and lunged for her, but the sheriff held him by the arm and yanked him back.

"Here now, boy, you hold on," he yelled.

"What's happening, Sheriff?" Jake asked, stepping forward.

"I'm not quite sure, Jake. I stopped this fella for running a red light in town. He didn't have a license, and he acted mighty strange. I decided to take him in, just to be on the safe side, but he asked me to bring him here. Said a Miss Camille Henderson could clear everything up."

Jake stared at the man, as everyone did, and called over his shoulder without looking back, "Camille? Can you identify this man?"

"Yes, I can. He's Clay Nettles, my ex-fiancé and a thief."

"Camille, wait! I can explain!" The man lunged forward again.

"Stop that!" the sheriff roared.

"I need to talk to her. Alone. Then everything will be cleared up."

Camille studied her ex-fiancé and wondered what she'd ever seen in him. They hadn't dated that long before her father's sudden death. She supposed she'd been so off balance, she hadn't had good judgment. "I don't want to talk to you."

"Camille, please. It will be in your best interest." In spite of the forty-degree temperature, Clay was sweating.

"No, thank you." She wasn't even tempted.

"Maybe you should hear what he has to say," a male voice said.

Camille spun around and stared at Griffin Randall. "Why?"

"Curiosity, I guess," he said with a slight smile.

"Very well," Camille agreed, turning back to face Clay. "He can have his say, but not alone."

"Camille, please, I can't speak in front of all these people," Clay insisted.

Griffin stepped up behind Camille. She could sense his warmth, and it sent shivers over her body. His gruff voice wasn't talking to her, however. "You heard the lady. Either speak your piece or get out of here."

Apparently Clay realized he wasn't going to sway Griff or her. He leaned toward Camille in a futile attempt to get closer. "Look, Camille, I made a mistake. But I thought you were going to break our engagement. I just wanted to get your attention. I didn't have any intention of *keeping* your money. You've got to believe me."

Camille was amazed. Suddenly, the tragedy had turned into a farce. "Clay, even a five-year-old wouldn't believe that story."

He flushed. "Okay, but if you have me arrested, it will take years before you get your money. That's why I'm here. We can work this out. You drop the charges, and I'll return most of your money."

"Most?" she returned.

"If you don't agree, you'll regret it." His voice turned hard, bitter. "I'll tie it up in every appeals court I can find. I'll prove you gave me permission to take it because you loved me. I'll—''

Griffin's hand came down on her shoulder, but she didn't wait for him to help her out. "Clay, I don't care what you do. Eventually, you'll end up in prison, and that will be very satisfying to me. Sheriff, there's a warrant out for this man's arrest. The FBI is looking for him.''

Then she turned and walked back to the house.

"Camille, you bitch, you'll live to regret—"

His words wouldn't have made her turn around. But the sudden cessation of his words, accompanied by a thud, had her spinning around in time to see Clay fall to the ground, with Griffin standing over him, his hands clenched in fists.

"Well, now, boy, that weren't necessary, but I guess I understand,'' the sheriff said as he hauled Clay to his feet and shoved him into the back of the squad car again. "I'll get this piece of dirt into town and call the FBI. Sorry if I disturbed you, Jake.''

"No problem, Sheriff.''

After the car tore back down the driveway, Red spoke. "Let's eat lunch before it gets cold.''

LUNCH WAS ALMOST OVER before anyone spoke.

"Do you suppose your ex-fiancé really thought he could convince you not to press charges?'' Janie asked.

"I guess so,'' Camille said with a laugh. "Though how could he have known the FBI had found him when they only froze the accounts this morning? We're a long way from Chicago.''

"Probably his friend Reilly let him know there was a problem last night," Griffin said as he took a bite of pie.

Chad asked a question, but Camille didn't hear his words. Instead, she turned to Griffin. "How did you know the name of Clay's friend in Chicago?"

Everyone at the table fell silent, their attention turning to Griffin. He froze, saying nothing.

"Griff?"

Jake spoke up. "I think I may have mentioned the man's name to Griff, Camille. I thought he might know him."

Griff let out a sigh, but Camille continued to stare at him. "I might believe that, Jake, if Griff didn't look so guilty. And if you'd gone to your office to fax all that information you got. But you went upstairs, straight to Griff's sickbed, didn't you?"

"I asked him to," Griff admitted. "I thought maybe I could help."

"So the FBI didn't find my money. You did?"

He nodded. "You've taken care of me while I was sick. I wanted to—"

"Pay me back?" she asked, her heart aching. He couldn't even accept a little nursing from her.

"I owed you," he muttered.

Camille got up and left the room without saying anything. She didn't want repayment. She wanted his love. *Silly girl*, she chastised herself. He'd warned her again and again.

What was she going to do now?

Megan tapped on the door and opened it simultaneously. "Cammy, are you all right?"

She pasted on a smile on her stiff lips. "Of course. Was I rude? Sorry, I was a little upset, but I'm fine now."

"You're sure? You haven't seemed too happy to get some of your money back. Was it Clay who upset you?"

Camille gave a half laugh. "No. That man means nothing to me now. I don't know what I saw in him."

"Good. I'm glad Griff beaned him."

"Yeah. Me, too, even if it means I owe him even more."

"Oh, honey, you can't worry about owing Griff. He helped you because—"

"Because he owed me for nursing him."

Megan grinned. "I know that's what he says, but I think he helped you because he cares about you."

Camille's heart lurched in hope before it settled back to its steady beat. "I don't think so."

"Well, things are looking up with the return of some of your money. So maybe other good things will happen, too," Megan suggested. "Want to go into town with me this afternoon? I could use some help in the store, and you're very good with the antiques."

"I love them. Once I thought about opening an antique store when I go home. But now I've decided to study business, learn to handle my finances without having to rely of some scumbag like Clay.''

"Oh, Cammy, don't talk about leaving yet. Maybe you could be my partner? That would be great.''

Camille only smiled. She knew that wouldn't work. Because Griffin would be here.

She couldn't stay.

SOMETHING WAS WRONG.

Griffin knew he'd more than paid Camille back for her nursing care. At least in dollars and cents. A lot of nursing could be hired for a half-million dollars.

But he wasn't satisfied with what had happened. Maybe it was Camille's reaction.

He'd shifted back to the bedroom by the kitchen, so Brett and Anna's room could be completely cleaned by Mavis and Ethel, and Jake had left his laptop beside the bed for him. Though he was tired, he didn't feel sleepy.

Perhaps he should check the market. The past couple of days he'd focused on Camille's problem. He hadn't even checked the stock he'd placed all their money in just before he came down with the chicken pox.

At least if he lost any of Camille's money on the stock, it wouldn't matter much. Which took off some of the pressure he'd felt.

When he called up the numbers, he stared at them, finding them difficult to believe. He'd expected a sudden upswing, but the stock had soared beyond his hopes.

"Jake!" he yelled, hoping his cousin was still in the kitchen.

Jake popped his head through the open door. "Yeah? You need something?"

"Nope. Just want to let you know I made everyone some money."

"Everyone?"

"You asked me to invest a hundred thousand of the corporation money. I bought this stock," he said, pointing to a New York Stock Exchange symbol going by.

"The one selling at fifty-seven?" Jake asked. "How much did you pay for it?"

"Five dollars," Griff said, grinning. "I'd recommend selling now. I don't think it will go up much more."

"Five?" Jake said. "Five? Hell, you made us a lot of money!"

"Yeah. And Camille, too. I invested fifty thousand for her."

Jake stared at him. "Camille let you invest in the stock market for her?"

Griff understood his amazement. "Well, not really. I tried to talk her into it, but she refused. Said something about becoming a stockbroker herself so she wouldn't have to trust anyone."

"Ah. That sounds about right. So how did you—?"

"I set up an account for her and put my money in it."

"So she just pays you back the fifty thousand and gets to keep the profit? That's nice of you, Griff."

He shrugged his shoulders. He wasn't sure being nice was his motivation.

Jake returned to the subject at hand. "Yeah, sell. I'm not going to go against your advice."

"Would you ask Camille about selling, too?" Griff asked, keeping his gaze on the computer screen.

"I'll do even better than that," Jake promised. "I'll tell her she has to give the order to you personally."

"Jake!" Griff yelled, but Jake was already out the door.

Damn, he didn't want to see Camille alone. *Like hell you don't want to see her alone!* Okay, okay, so he did. But he shouldn't.

A knock sounded on the door.

"Come in."

Camille opened the door but didn't move into the room. "Jake said you invested money for me. I told you no and I didn't give you any money, so whatever you did, it's yours." She turned to leave.

"Wait!" he called. He held his breath until she came back into view. "Look, you're not going to be able to touch the money the FBI recovered for a few months. You'll need some money."

"I'll find a job."

"You're leaving the ranch?"

"Of course I'm leaving. I can't live off Megan and Chad forever." She kept her gaze averted.

"Take the money, Cammy. I want you to have it. You'll have over two hundred thousand after you return my fifty thousand to me."

"No."

"But you waited on me. I—"

"Don't say it!" she yelled at him, taking him by surprise.

"Say what?"

"That you owe me! You don't *owe* me. I took care of you because— I mean, you're family. I took care of you, as I would any other family member. I don't need you to pay me."

"I'm not used to taking favors," he returned stiffly.

"Too bad."

"Okay. I helped you out because you're family," he said, narrowing his gaze, waiting to see if his turnabout-fair-play worked.

She opened her mouth to protest, then stopped.

"You were going to say I'm not family, weren't you?" he asked, grinning. "But that's the excuse you used."

"Yes, but I believe it. To you it's just an excuse."

"You can't use two standards." Then his voice softened. "Please, Cammy, take the money. It's not costing me anything."

"You'll take out the initial investment?"

"And charge you a brokerage fee, okay?"

"Okay," she agreed with a sigh. "And thank you."

"My pleasure." Then she disappeared from the door. He'd made a lot of money in his lifetime, both for himself and others. He'd never had anyone react the way Camille had.

THE IRONY OF IT ALL. She'd come to Megan's home because she'd lost almost all her money. Now she felt she had to leave because she'd gotten so much of it back.

Even if Clay managed to tie up the money he took, she still had a large sum of money, thanks to Griffin, to last her several years if she wasn't terribly extravagant. She couldn't continue to drift, with no goals.

She'd been half-joking when she told Griff she would become a stockbroker, but the more she thought about it, the more she wanted to go back to school. She didn't want to turn her money over to someone else again. And she might find it interesting to help other women learn about finances, providing advice and investing for them.

Besides, there wasn't a need for her to stay. She'd been helpful with the babies, she knew. But everything was returning to normal. All the family would be home with Brett and Anna's arrival tonight. Mavis and Ethel were working out well.

No one needed her.

And they all wanted Griffin to stay.

She had to leave. After all, Griffin had made it

clear he wasn't interested in her. In spite of what Megan had said. Camille closed her eyes. She wanted to believe Megan was right. She and Griffin had grown close, caring for the children. Then, when he'd teased her for kisses while he was sick, she'd thought he'd changed his mind.

She wanted what Megan had. And she'd found her own Randall. But now she'd be alone the rest of her life. Because she'd discovered she had something in common with Megan's husband and his brothers. She was a one-man woman, as they were one-woman men.

Her shoulders slumped, and one tear trailed down her face. She would go away and—

As if she actually heard his voice, she remembered her father yelling at her when she was younger and had become discouraged. "Hendersons are not quitters!"

With a half sob, she looked upward. "But, Dad, he doesn't want me."

There was no answer, as she'd known there wouldn't be. But her father's words stayed with her. She hadn't put up much of a fight, it was true. Should she give Griff one more chance? Could she force him to reconsider his withdrawal?

If not, at least she would leave knowing she hadn't been a quitter.

DINNER WAS a lengthy affair as all the Randalls, Red and Mildred, Griffin and Camille exchanged stories of the past few days.

Except that Camille scarcely said anything.

Griffin answered any questions that were asked about their dealing with the children on their own. And sneaked a look at Camille each time. She concentrated on her meal, never looking up.

"Camille and Griff, Brett and I brought you back special gifts from San Francisco, to thank you for taking such good care of Torie," Anna announced.

"That's not necessary," Griff hurriedly said.

"But of course it is, Griffin," Camille suddenly said. "You, more than anyone, understand about repaying people for their kindness."

An awkward silence fell. Camille seemed to realize her words were out of place. She looked at Anna. "I didn't really mean that, Anna. It's a private joke between Griff and me. It was very thoughtful of you to buy us something."

Griff stared at her. A private joke? They had no private jokes, and she knew it. Her words had been a jab at him.

"We bought Griff a painting of the Golden Gate Bridge," Brett said, a smile on his face.

"And Camille? What did you bring her?" Janie asked.

Anna giggled. "You remember that store you were interested in after you and Pete got married?" Anna asked. "The one we bought B.J. a present from? Well, I found one even better in San Francisco." Anna laughed again.

Griff stared around the table as all four Randall wives broke into laughter. "What kind of store?"

"Oh, I don't think I should tell," Anna said.

"What are they talking about, Jake?" Griff demanded.

"I don't have any idea."

B.J. grinned at her husband. "And we don't intend to tell you."

"Well, let's have these presents out for everyone to see," Jake suggested. "We've all finished our dessert."

"No, Camille gets hers in private," Anna said.

"Brett, you know what's going on?" Jake asked.

Griff studied Brett as his cheeks flushed.

"Uh, I promised Anna I wouldn't say anything. I didn't even look," he said, shooting an apologetic look to Camille, who seemed as puzzled as everyone else.

"Come upstairs with us, Camille," Anna said, jumping up. "We'll show you your gift now."

All the women, even Mildred, hurried from the room.

As soon as the door closed behind them, the rest of the men turned to Brett. Jake led the questioning. "What were they talking about, Brett?"

"I promised Anna."

"But, Brett, we won't tell on you."

He stubbornly shook his head.

"But we don't keep secrets around here," Jake protested.

"Sure, we do," Brett contradicted. "Just usually no one knows we're keeping secrets, so it's not a problem."

ANNA'S GIFT, a shockingly sheer peignoir set in pale blue that looked good with Camille's eyes, was beautiful. "It's— I've never seen anything so beautiful, Anna, but where will I wear it? I mean—"

The ladies all burst into laughter again.

Finally, Anna said, "We expect you to wear it on your honeymoon, sweetie."

"But I'm not getting married," Camille assured them.

"Then you'd better hide from Griff," B.J. warned with a laugh. "I was afraid he'd take a bite out of you instead of his dinner, the way he was looking at you."

Camille flushed. "He may be interested in—in sex, but he's not at all interested in marriage."

"They never are," Janie assured her.

"Well, thank you for—for the present, Anna. But I enjoyed taking care of Torie. And all the babies. Now, if you'll excuse me, I'm rather tired." Hoping to escape before her tears fell, Camille scooped up the peignoir set and ran from the room.

"Did we upset her?" Anna asked in a small voice.

"I don't know," Megan said. "But you remember how it is when you're not sure he loves you. Maybe Griff will change her mood tomorrow."

"Maybe we should all enlist our husbands' help," B.J. said. "No sense in prolonging the misery."

The four wives nodded, then went to their respective bedrooms for a loving talk with their husbands.

CAMILLE SAT ON HER BED, staring at the gift. It was perfect for her plans, if she had the nerve.

And she did.

She'd promised herself she'd pull out all the stops to prove to Griffin that he loved her. The peignoir set was definitely perfect, unless it was overkill.

She paced the room for half an hour, debating her choices. Finally, she gathered the peignoir set, bikini panties and her favorite perfume and retreated to the connecting bath.

Half an hour later, she stared at herself in the mirror. Blue was the perfect color for her. She knew she'd get Griff's attention.

With a sigh, she sat down on her bed and stared at the clock. She had to wait at least an hour before the household would've gone to bed.

She must've changed her mind ten times in the next hour, but when the clock said she'd waited long enough, she got up from the bed, checked her appearance one more time, then shrugged on her terry-cloth robe over the peignoir set.

Opening her door very slowly, she slipped into the semidarkened hallway, praying she wouldn't run into any of the Randalls. When she reached the kitchen, she breathed a sigh of relief. Red and Mildred were back in their house, so she should be home free.

She tiptoed across the kitchen, rehearsing her speech. She hoped he wouldn't slam the door in her face. But she wasn't sure. After all, he didn't appear to be a man interested in emotions. Especially hers.

Even if he rejected her afterward…she'd at least have memories that would have to suffice for the rest of her life.

She knocked on Griffin's door and threw off the terry-cloth robe.

Chapter Fifteen

Griffin lay stretched out on his bed, thinking.

He didn't like the way Camille had reacted to the events of the day. And he was afraid she was going to leave. Because he'd gotten her money back for her.

"Damn," he muttered wearily.

He couldn't think of any way to stop her from going, without committing himself, and he was sure that would be a mistake. He didn't know how to make a relationship work. And if he married her and then she left him, he didn't think he could face the pain.

A knock on the door disturbed him. Maybe Jake found out about Camille's gift and wanted to share with him. He pulled on sweatpants and opened his door.

He couldn't believe his eyes.

But his body could. Already he was responding to the vision of Camille standing before him in a see-through robe and gown that showed all her delicious curves to advantage.

Was he dreaming?

"Camille?" he asked even as his arms reached for her.

"I've decided to be honest with you."

Her words stopped him cold, something he wouldn't have believed possible ten seconds earlier.

"I don't understand." At least he hoped he didn't.

"I—I've pretended I didn't care for you. But it's not true. I love you."

He tried to speak—he really did. But all that came out was a strangled noise.

She held up her hand, which shifted a few other body parts that held his attention. "Don't worry. I know you don't want commitment or—or a future, but I want one night. I want to love you just this once."

"This once?" he questioned, unable to get out anything else.

"Yes," she assured him, and moved to press herself against him. Her lips lifted to his as her arms went around his neck. When they touched, the same lightning bolt of feeling surged through him, as it always had.

But before he could go down for the count, so lost in the sensations she stirred in him, her words ran through his mind. Breaking off the kiss was one of the hardest things he'd ever done, but he couldn't—

"Wait!" he ordered as she pressed forward. "Wait, Camille. I don't— I told you I'm not a family man, like Jake and the others. I don't want to mislead you.''

She briefly buried her face on his shoulder. Then she bravely looked him in the eye. "I know."

He tried to slow his body's response to her touch, but he wasn't making much progress. "Are you sure this is what you want?"

"This is what I want. I want the memory of having loved you when I leave," she said softly.

He didn't want to hear that she was leaving, even though he had every intention of doing so. But he wanted to know she was safe and happy here with the Randalls. Why did it matter to him? he asked himself.

And he didn't like the answer. Camille was different from all the other women in his life. So different that it frightened him. Did he love her? And even if he did, would it make a difference? He'd said he wasn't cut out for family life, for love, for commitment.

Would he even have a choice once he made love to Camille? And that was the reason panic filled him. He didn't know the answer to that question.

His body seemed overly sensitive, like a Geiger counter, quivering in response to her touch. Was it already too late? Even now, he couldn't tell her to go away. His body wouldn't obey his commands to let her go.

Was it because of the other Randall men's marriages? Would it make a difference if he'd met Camille in Chicago, without the influence of his cousins? He stared down into her big blue eyes and unconsciously shook his head no.

"No?" she said, tears filling her eyes.

"I didn't say no," he returned, holding her tighter.

"You shook your head."

"I was thinking of something else," he whispered as his lips descended to hers. He could wait no longer. Self-examination could come later, much later. Already he'd exhausted himself trying to back away from what he desperately wanted. No more discussion.

Pulling her into his room, he closed the door, then wrapped his arms around her, his lips covering hers, devouring them. He'd wanted her since he'd first seen her, the hunger growing with each passing day.

Now she was his.

It wasn't far to the bed, but by the time they'd reached it, their lips never parting, they had both shed their clothes. Now the sexy covering was gone. All that was left was her satiny skin, her silky hair, her soft lips.

"Cammy," he whispered as his lips left hers to caress her bare breasts.

Her hands were touching him, and he trembled beneath her fingertips. He'd never experienced such a disturbing reaction to a woman, such a complete domination of his senses. His lips returned to hers as if he hadn't tasted them in a decade, the hunger growing and growing.

"Griff, love me," she whispered, urging him on when he needed no urging.

When he entered her, the frenzy increased, making thought impossible. But a sense of fulfillment, of completion seized him, something he'd never experienced before. A coming home that filled a secret need deep within him.

Then sensation took over, and the two of them were locked in a mind-blowing, total consumption that, when it ended, left him exhausted and unable to focus, though there was something very important on the edge of consciousness.

Then he forgot.

CAMILLE HAD TEARS in her eyes.

She hadn't realized just how breathtakingly beautiful their moments together would be. Or how much the thought of leaving him would hurt.

"Griff, I—I love you," she whispered, repeating what he didn't want to hear, unable to hold back those words. His face was buried in her hair, and she waited, scarcely breathing, for him to once again remind her that he wasn't looking for commitment.

Nothing.

With a sob, she added, "I know you warned me, but I couldn't help myself. You're the other part of me that I've searched for. If—if you don't want me, I won't— I'll go away, but I wanted you to know."

When he didn't move this time, she reached up to those powerful arms and grasped them, giving him a little shove. He shifted off her body slightly, but he said nothing.

"Griff, look, I don't expect hearts and flowers—" though her heart yearned for them "—but I think you could at least say something."

He snored.

Her eyes widened in shock. She gave him a mighty shove and half sat up as he rolled off her. How could he? He made shameless, glorious love to her, the most incredible experience in her life, and he was asleep?

"Griff!"

No response, as if he was dead to the world. Another snore assured her he was alive. But even when she shook him, he didn't wake up.

Then she remembered that he was still in the recuperative stages of chicken pox. He'd gotten up for lunch for the first time in over a week, then gone back to bed for the afternoon.

She must've drained any energy he had with their lovemaking. It certainly hadn't been easy and gentle. More like explosive and—and incredible. But with him still in the throes of chicken pox, she guessed she couldn't complain at his passing out.

She slipped from the bed and picked up the peignoir set and the panties, folding them neatly, then retrieved her terry-cloth robe from the hall. About to slip into it, she stared at Griff's sleeping form.

Why should she deny herself the pleasure of staying with him for a while longer? She wanted to share his bed so badly, to hold him against her, to fill her senses with him, knowing that it would be the only time.

It was her father's insistence that she give it her all that had her dropping the robe and sliding beneath the covers, taking the warm, muscular body of the man she loved into her arms.

He hadn't heard her last declaration of love.

But he hadn't rejected her even before. Until he did, hurt her beyond belief, sent her out of his life, she was going to do what her father had said. She wasn't going to quit.

Amazing how wonderful such gritty advice was, she thought as she snuggled against his broad, hairy chest, rested her forehead against his scratchy chin, felt his soft breath in her hair.

And prayed she'd never have to leave his embrace.

STILL IN A VACATION MODE, the Randalls sat around the breakfast table the next morning, having a second cup of coffee. Even B.J. wasn't rushing out to do her rounds.

"Man, it feels good to have us all together again," Jake said, looking over at the children playing in the playpens. Toby had already left for school, but everyone else was there.

"Do you think I should go wake up Camille? She doesn't usually sleep this late," Megan suggested.

"She's probably enjoying a morning free of children," Janie said. "I know I did, when we were in

Hawaii, and I'm their mother. Poor Camille deserves to sleep late.''

There was a general nod and agreement. Pete asked Jake about the work for the day, as if signaling an end to their laziness. Before Jake could respond, they heard a car drive up.

''Visitors this early? Maybe it's the sheriff,'' Chad suggested.

''Nope, I don't think so. The FBI came to town and got Nettles before supper last night,'' Jake said. ''I don't think—''

A knock on the back door ended any speculation. Mildred opened the door and invited their guest in. Bill Haney, looking apprehensive but determined, entered the kitchen.

Jake stood. ''Howdy, Haney. Come sit down.''

''No. I—I need to see Griffin.''

Jake frowned. ''He's not up yet. You know he's been sick. I said I'll tell you when—''

''He was well enough to knock a fella down yesterday. You're trying to protect him from me, but—''

Red came around the table. ''Now, don't get all upset, Bill. If Jake said he'd let you know, then he'll let you know.''

Haney, obviously recognizing a sympathetic note in Red's voice, turned to him. ''You don't understand, Red. I know you don't have a high opinion of me, but I can't stand the strain. I have to tell him.''

''Tell him what?'' Red asked.

"That I'm his father," Haney said, before swallowing like a man crossing the desert without water.

While Pete and Jake had known, they hadn't divulged that information to the rest of the family. A shocked silence filled the room.

Finally, after staring at the man, Red turned to Jake. "I think you'd better see if Griff's awake." Then he led Haney over to a seat at the table and poured him a cup of coffee.

With a sigh, Jake rose. He didn't like the idea of springing Haney on Griffin so early in the morning, while he was still recuperating. But what choice did Jake have?

He walked down the short hall to Griffin's room, rapped on the door and pulled it open.

"Griff, you need to— Uh-oh!"

CAMILLE MUST'VE BEEN on the edge of sleep before Jake's noisy arrival, because she came awake at once with the rapping on the door. But she couldn't make any movement to prevent being discovered naked in Griff's arms.

There wasn't time.

But there was time to see Griff open his eyes, see Jake at the door and then stare in horror at her.

Horror.

As in he wished he'd never seen her.

And certainly not naked in his bed.

Well, she'd wanted an answer. There it was. She'd forced herself on him last night. And like any red-blooded American man, he wasn't turning down free sex, but he didn't want anything to do with the morning after.

After Jake slammed the door closed, she reached for her terry-cloth robe as she slid from the bed.

"Camille, wait, don't go!"

She ignored him.

Oh, he was a gentleman. But she'd seen his honest reaction. All the polite words he could spout wouldn't change what he felt.

And those polite words wouldn't change what was going to happen now. She was going to leave. With a broken heart that would last her the rest of her life. Just like the love she felt for Griffin Randall. He would always be a part of her.

Without looking at him, she circled the bed while she tied a knot in the sash that held the robe closed. She had to get away before she broke down into tears and pathetically begged him to love her.

He'd warned her. Over and over again. It wasn't his fault that she loved him and wanted to believe he could love her.

She had to get out of there.

Swinging open the door, she charged out of his room, ignoring his desperate call, right into the kitchen.

If she'd run into a plate-glass window, she couldn't have been more shocked. The entire family, except Toby, was staring at her, their mouths opened, their eyes widened.

With a sob, she tore into a run, streaming past her

beloved friends as if they were demons, chasing her.

She had to get away.

SHOCKED SILENCE FILLED the kitchen.

Then Megan jumped to her feet. "I have to go see about Camille."

The other ladies immediately followed suit. "We're coming, too," B.J. added. "Jake, watch the kids."

As soon as the kitchen was empty of all females, except for Elizabeth, Caroline and Torie, who showed no interest in the bizarre goings-on of the adults, silence fell again.

Finally, Bill Haney said, "What's going on? Are you going to wake up Griffin or not?"

Jake cleared his throat. "I think Griff is awake now. I'll just, uh, just check with him about coming out."

"Yeah, he may not be up to it," Brett said with a chuckle that earned a glare from his older brother.

As Jake turned away, Chad whispered, "I think you brought Griff two presents from San Francisco instead of just one."

Brett grinned in return.

EVEN AS QUICKLY as they followed, the ladies found Camille already in the shower, so they settled down on the two chairs and the bed to wait for her emergence.

"Do you think he seduced her?" Megan whispered.

B.J. shrugged. "I don't know. But I'm sure he didn't force her. After all, he's a Randall."

"But we don't really know— I mean, he's only been here a few weeks," Megan argued, worried about Camille.

"Jake trusts him," B.J. returned.

They sat in silence. Who could argue with that remark?

The bathroom door opened, and Camille gasped as she faced the Randall female contingent unexpectedly. She was wrapped in a towel, even her hair wet. "What—what are you doing here?" she demanded, her cheeks flushing.

"We want to know if you're all right," Megan said, hurrying to her side. "He didn't hurt you, did he?"

Camille closed her eyes, then opened them, hoping tears wouldn't fall. "No, of course not."

"But he seduced you?" Janie asked.

"No." Camille spoke clearly. She wasn't going to blame Griffin for her troubles. "No, I seduced him. With your gift from San Francisco," she added, looking at Anna.

"Oh. Good for you," Anna said with a big smile.

Camille acted as if she'd been slapped. "Good for me? You approve?"

B.J. chuckled. "When you live in glass houses...you know?"

"But I shouldn't have—"

"Why did you?" Megan asked softly.

Camille debated her answers. But in the end, there was only one. "I love him."

"And that's the only reason we approve," Anna assured her. "We've all been there, sweetie. Sometimes all you can do is love them."

Camille sagged against the door frame. "You don't understand. He warned me, again and again, that he would never marry, never love—"

"They all do that," Mildred said, chuckling. "Well, not Red," she added. "That man was marriage minded from day one, but that's because he's older, more mature than these boys. They don't understand what's best for them."

Then the tears fell. Camille couldn't help it. They were all so wonderful, standing there trying to comfort her, believing everything would work out for her and Griff, when she knew it wouldn't.

"He—he doesn't ever want to see me again."

"He said that?" Megan demanded, her hackles rising.

"Not in words, but—but," she sobbed, "he looked at me like that." She relived that look in her mind, knowing she would never be able to forget the piercing pain when she gave up her fantasies about a future with Griff.

Apparently, she'd convinced her audience of the hopelessness of her situation because silence fell. Finally, Janie asked, "What are you going to do?"

Camille swallowed. "I have to leave. He said—" She came to an abrupt halt. No, he hadn't said. He'd called to her. He'd asked her to wait, but she'd run away.

She forgot all about the women in her room, women she'd come to love and respect. All she could think about was her disorderly retreat this morning. She hadn't done what her father said. She'd run.

She whirled back around to face the others. "He didn't tell me to go away. He called for me to wait."

"Why didn't you?"

"Because I was embarrassed. Because I'm a coward."

Megan jumped to her feet and hugged Camille. "Don't be silly. You're not a coward."

"I am if I don't make Griff tell me to my face to go away," Camille slowly said, her gaze fastened on the window, as she stared out at the mountains.

"Good plan," Megan assured her, and the others nodded.

Camille started for the door, then stopped and looked down at herself. "Maybe I'd better dress first. I've made enough appearances today in my bathrobe."

"Yeah," B.J. said. "We'll make sure Griffin is still around when you're ready."

The ladies left Camille's room.

"Should we have told her about Mr. Haney?" Anna asked as they descended the stairs.

"I think maybe we should leave that to Griff. But I hope that information doesn't drive him away before he has a chance to realize how much Camille is offering him," Megan said with a sigh.

Chapter Sixteen

Griffin searched for his sweatpants as he searched for his sanity. The morning was starting at a faster pace than he could handle.

As he found them, thrown on the floor a few feet from the bed, he remembered how they got there, how Camille had ended up in his bed. He stared into space, remembering even more how incredible their loving had been.

How much he needed to find Camille.

The look on her face as she ran from the room scared him. Did she hate him because he hadn't been able to resist her? Did she think he'd made love to her without loving her?

At least that much was clear to him now. He might not know much about being a family man, but he was ready to learn. Whatever it took, he wasn't going to let Camille get away.

He almost fell to his knees at that thought.

"Uh, Griff...?" Jake called from the door.

He spun around and thought he was losing his balance.

"Easy there, cuz. Are you all right?"

Griff covered his face with his hands. Then he looked at Jake. "I will be. I need to find Camille."

"Uh, well, I'm sorry about interrupting earlier. But Bill Haney is here." Jake leaned over and picked up a T-shirt from a chair, handing it to Griff. "Put this on."

Jake's order made sense, when nothing else did, so Griff put on the T-shirt, along with his sweatpants. "I gotta find Camille," he repeated.

Jake ran a hand through his hair. "Well, now, Griff, not just yet."

"Why? I didn't intend to hurt her. I have to explain. She was upset when—"

"I know. And she won't leave until you talk to her."

"Leave? She's leaving?" Griff started for the door, willing to run over Jake if he didn't get out of his way. He couldn't let Camille leave.

"Hold it, Griff. We've got another problem."

"I can't let Camille leave, Jake. I can't." His strength seemed to have deserted him. His legs were trembling with weakness.

"We won't let Camille leave, I promise, if I have to hogtie her myself." He held Griff's shoulders and looked him in the eye. "I promise."

Griff slumped down, sitting on the edge of the bed. "Okay. Thanks, Jake."

Jake stood there, his hands on his hips, staring at him. Griff struggled to his feet. "I'm ready."

"Good. 'Cause Haney—"

"No, ready for Camille. She—"

"We'll get to Camille. But you're going to have to deal with Haney first."

Griff felt even more confused than when he'd first awakened. Buying land held no significance until he'd set things straight with Camille. Things he hadn't understood until last night.

"Jake, Haney means nothing to me. You can—"

"No, Griff, I can't. I wish I could. Come with me and you'll understand." Jake took his arm and pulled him into the kitchen.

The children were playing quietly, as usual at the end of a meal. The Randall brothers and Red were sitting with coffee mugs in front of them. Griff immediately craved his own mug, filled with steaming, fragrant coffee.

And Bill Haney—at least Griff supposed the man was Bill Haney—sat beside Red, staring at him.

"Coffee, Red. He's gonna need it," Jake ordered, keeping his hand on Griff's arm, as if sensing how disoriented his cousin was.

Griff almost fell into his normal seat, at the end of the table beside Jake's place. When Red set the coffee in front of him, he muttered his thanks and brought it to his lips as if it were a potion that would give him life.

The hot liquid hit his stomach, and Griff drew a deep breath. His worried look went to the door. He knew Camille was somewhere upstairs.

He was distracted by Red setting a plate with biscuits and sausage in front of him. "Get some protein in you, boy. You're going to need your strength."

Everyone knew of his difficulties with Camille? Griff looked around him, receiving some sympathetic looks. Bill Haney left his seat by Red and moved down the table to sit across from him.

Just as he did so, the door opened and all the women returned to the table. Except Camille.

Jake cleared his throat, after everyone settled down again. "Uh, Griff, Haney has something to tell you. I hope you'll listen to him."

Griff stared at Jake and then the man across from him. What was going on? They insisted on talking about buying land now? The man seemed tense, even more tense than Griff himself.

"Okay," he muttered as he bit into a sausage-and-biscuit sandwich. He hated feeling this weak.

When nothing was said, he looked at the man across from him. "Mr. Haney?"

The man stiffened, then spoke abruptly. "I'm your father."

Griff stared at the man he never thought he'd meet, his mind spinning. Then he reacted. Standing up, he headed for his bedroom.

Jake grabbed his arm as he reached the door.

"Look, Griff, I know this is hard. But I'm asking you to let the man have his say. He came the day I got back, but I asked him to wait. I think both of you need to face this thing."

Griff didn't want to give in to Jake's pressure. He didn't want to face the man who had denied him even before he was born. But he wanted a life here in Wyoming, near his cousins.

He bowed his head, his hands on his hips, gathering his strength. Finally, he looked up at Jake. "Okay." The two of them came back to the table together.

He sat down and had to physically force his gaze to the man across from him. The first thing he noticed was the pain on the man's face. This meeting wasn't any easier for him than it was for Griff.

Good.

He sat there, stone-faced to hide his own pain, and waited.

"I knew you wouldn't want to know me. I screwed up a long time ago, and I've never stopped regretting it."

Just what he wanted to hear. Another rejection from his father. "Then let's just forget it," he said gruffly, and started to rise again, but Jake put his hand on his shoulder.

"Come on, Griff, give him a chance."

"Why? He didn't want me then and he doesn't want me now. What's the point?"

The man across from him half rose out of his chair. "Not want you? How can you think that? I've lived my life wondering every day where you were, how you were. Knowing my only son hated my guts."

"You didn't even know if my mother carried to term. Or whether I was a boy or a girl. You knew nothing."

"I knew," Haney said heavily. He turned to Jake. "I lied to your daddy. I did hear from Margaret. But my wife was still alive. I'd hurt her enough. I couldn't shame her. She hadn't deserved it."

"So you didn't respond to my mother? You left a seventeen-year-old pregnant on her own?" Griff asked bitterly, his lips curled in contempt.

Bill Haney straightened his shoulders. "I never lied to your mother. I told her I couldn't divorce Grace. She said she didn't care. But I did what I could. I sent her all the savings we had."

Griff was stunned. "You sent her money?" In all her talk about his father, his mother had never mentioned that fact.

"A lot of money. Then, after—after Grace died, I contacted Margaret. I asked her to marry me. She wouldn't. Said there was another man. Wouldn't even let me see you." The man's shoulders slumped again.

There was a tense silence as Griff tried to take in all the information being thrown at him this morning. His mother had lied to him. Had denied him his father, because she'd wanted revenge for Bill's earlier rejection. How easily Griff could believe that about his mother. She'd been that bitter.

And how sad that she'd denied herself the love of her family, the love of the father of her child, because she was proud and bitter.

"So she told you about me?" he finally asked, his voice hoarse.

"She gave me a copy of your birth certificate.

And asked for more money. But she wouldn't let me see you.''

Griffin folded his hands and laid his head on them.

''Look, Griffin, I'm not asking you to forgive me. I betrayed my wife because I fell in love with your mother. And I've lived a lonely, bitter life as payment. But—but I couldn't live here, with you nearby, and not tell you. Besides, when I'm gone, you would know. I figured it would be cowardly not to face you before I go.''

A small measure of respect slipped under Griff's defenses. Then something the man had said bothered him. ''What do you mean, when you're gone I'll know.''

''I changed my will after Grace died. I left everything to you.''

''I don't want it!'' Griff roared, his mother's teachings still a force in him.

Bill Haney, now that he'd told his story, seemed stronger. He stared at Griffin, a sympathetic look on his face. ''Don't matter, boy. It's yours. You have no choice in the matter.''

Griff glared at him, but Red got up from the end of the table and came to sit beside Bill Haney. ''I think I've wronged you, Bill.''

To everyone's surprise, it was Bill who argued against Red's overture. ''No, Red. I've screwed up my life and several others. You haven't wronged me. And I can't do much to make amends. But I've got to try.''

Griff stared at him.

Haney stood and nodded his head at Griff. "I've had my say, and I appreciate you listening. If—if you have any questions, or want to see the place, let me know. You'll be welcome." He turned to go without waiting for an answer.

Griff found it difficult to take it all in. But he'd learned a lot since he'd come to live with the Randalls. Family was important. And his mother wasn't as innocent as she'd portrayed herself to be. And this man wasn't as black as he'd thought him.

"Wait." His voice was hoarse, weak, but Bill Haney heard him, turning around, a faint hope rising in his eyes.

No one spoke.

Finally, Griff spoke again. "I can't— I don't— What do you want from me?"

Haney took one step back toward the table. "Nothing, except maybe to speak, to talk once in a while. I won't tell no one I'm your daddy, I promise. But maybe, if you don't mind, I could call you. Not often. I won't make a pest of myself, I promise. But—"

Griff couldn't bear the man's pitiful appeal any longer. He stood and extended his hand. "I can't promise— Okay, we'll get to know each other."

Bill Haney's face lit up with a smile like none the Randalls had ever seen. He clasped Griff's hand with both of his and clung to it, nodding his head over and over again. "I'm so grateful, so grateful. I won't tell anyone, I promise. I—"

"Telling people is up to you, Mr.—Bill," Griff said, giving in to the tug on his heart. "But I'll still go by the name of Randall. It's too late in my life to change my name."

Haney was still clinging to Griff's hand, still nodding his head, but a look of wonder came into his eyes as Griff's words penetrated. "I—I can tell people you're my son? You won't be ashamed—I mean, I can tell?"

Griff didn't answer, looking at Jake for some help.

"Hell, all these chatterboxes already know," Jake said, smiling. "No point in trying to keep it quiet." He sent his brothers and Red a silent apology, hoping they'd understand he was trying to ease the tension.

Griff tugged gently on his hand, and Bill released it reluctantly.

"Do you—do you think you might want to see my place? I kind of let it go these last couple of years, but it's a nice place. I could move into town and give it to you now if you want—I mean, ask Jake. He was wantin' to buy it. It's a sweet piece of land."

"You just saved us a lot of money, Bill," Jake said. "We were buying it for Griff. He's a horseman. You should see him with some of Pete's wild stock. He tames them."

Bill's eyes lit up. "Like your mama. She could wind any horse around her little finger." His joy dimmed. "And any man, too."

Suddenly, Griffin could take no more. He stood on his shaky legs. "I have to get out of here," he muttered, and headed for the back door.

He needed to be alone. To consider all that had happened. His life was turned upside down, both from his realization that Camille mattered more than anyone in his life, and the discovery of his father and the lies his mother told.

He headed for the corral.

CAMILLE HAD DRESSED and dried her hair, put on makeup with shaky fingers. She wanted to look her best. It strengthened her courage. She was ashamed of her panic that morning, and she was going to make sure she made every effort to find her happiness. Like her father said.

Griffin was going to have to face her and tell her he cared nothing about her.

She came down the stairs, her chin up, and shoved on the kitchen door. Just in time to hear Griffin tell everyone he was leaving.

Her heart sank.

She caught a glimpse of him storming out the back door, in jeans and a T-shirt and house shoes. He was leaving in his house shoes?

She stared at the frozen scene before her. No one was moving. What was going on?

"Is Griff leaving now?" she finally asked, looking at Megan.

"Not really leaving. He just needed some time to

think," Megan assured her. "At least, that's what I think."

"What happened?"

A man she'd met once before, Haney, who owned the ranch next to the Randalls, stood. "He said he didn't mind."

His words did nothing to enlighten Camille. "I beg your pardon?"

"I'm his daddy. And he said it was okay."

No one said anything.

"Poor Griff," Camille finally muttered. "No wonder—"

"I promised I wouldn't be a bother," Haney hurriedly added.

Red stood up and put an arm around him. "A'course you did, Bill. It's just that Griff needs time to take all this information in. It's not easy to discover that you've got a father, and that—that your mother lied to you."

Camille put a hand over her lips, to hold back the moan that was moving up her throat. Poor Griff, she thought again. Not only did he have her trying to make him change his mind about marriage. But he also had to deal with all this.

Even worse, she realized he wouldn't be able to stay here with the Randalls, as she'd hoped he would. Not with his father only a few miles away.

She'd lost. Without even getting to play her final card, she'd lost. The shock of this revelation would have Griff returning to Chicago, to a lonely existence.

Without saying a word, she turned and left the kitchen. Time to go pack.

JAKE ROSE FROM THE TABLE. "I'd better go see about Griff. Mr. Haney, maybe it would be better if you'd give Griff a little time to, uh, take everything in. He'll call you, in a day or two, okay?"

"Okay." The man nodded. "I won't tell anyone until I hear from him. I promise."

After Mr. Haney left, Jake looked at his wife. "What's up with Camille and Griff? Did you find out anything?"

"She loves him. But she doesn't know if he's interested," B.J. said.

"This won't help. We all know Griff wasn't prepared to be friendly with his father," Megan said. "He'll leave for sure, now."

Jake stared at his family. "Well, I for one don't intend to let him screw up his life like that."

"What are you going to do?" Chad asked.

"I'm going to go talk to Griff. Then we'll figure out a way of getting them together. After all, we're experts at matchmaking, aren't we?"

No one disagreed with him.

GRIFF LEANED against the corral, ignoring the bite of the cold air. His head was spinning with Haney's revelations. His father.

Living only a few miles away.

How could he—?

"Aren't you cold?" Jake asked.

He spun around, almost losing his balance. "What are you doing out here?" he growled.

"Trying to keep you from getting pneumonia." He draped a coat over Griff's shoulders. "And I thought we might talk a little."

"There's nothing to talk about."

"Oh, yeah, there is. Unless you want to lose all chance of happiness."

"I don't know what you mean."

"Yeah, you do. Remember the other day when B.J. and I were fighting?" Jake kept his gaze firmly on Griffin.

"Yeah."

"I almost made a stupid mistake."

"But everything's fine now," Griffin said hurriedly.

"Yeah, because one of my brothers came up with a good compromise. But I want you to know that nothing would've made me give up B.J. and Toby and Caroline. Nothing, even if I lost the battle. I know what's important in life. And I hope you do, too."

Griff knew. He'd discovered it last night in Camille's arms. Not sex. Love. A woman he couldn't walk away from, and didn't even want to try. Family.

He nodded.

"So you're not going to let Bill's announcement ruin your life, are you?"

"Ruin my life?"

"You're not going to run away, leaving Camille behind?"

"Of course not."

"You can live here, knowing your father is a few miles away?"

Trust Jake to get right to the point.

"I'm going to try. If Camille will— I don't know if she'll take me on. I've screwed up a few times, Jake."

Jake grimaced. "I did, too. I still do. Fortunately, women are good at forgiving us."

Griffin, after staring at his feet for several minutes, remembered his urgency earlier. "I'd better go find her. I think she might be planning on leaving."

As he turned toward the house, Jake put a hand on his shoulder. "You sure you want to go face that crowd?"

"What choice do I have? I'm not letting her get away."

"Well, from past experience, I know a place you can be real private."

"Where?"

Jake nodded toward the barn. "No one will bother you there. And there are some blankets in the tack room. Spread over some fresh hay, they make a real comfortable place for...whatever," he said with a grin.

"But if Camille is intent on leaving, she's not going to make a tour of the barn," Griff protested. "I'd better—"

"Trust me, I'll get her to the barn. And I'll lock the door until you convince her not to go."

Relief filled Griffin's face, and for the first time in a long while, he smiled.

CAMILLE HALTED her packing long enough to answer the knock on her bedroom door.

"Yes?" she said, swinging it open.

"You're leaving?" Megan said with a gasp, the other four ladies behind her.

"Megan, I have to. Besides, if I don't you know he will."

"All I know," Megan said, "is that Jake's got him in the barn and told us to get you down there. He's going to lock the two of you in the barn until you convince Griffin to stay."

She looked quite pleased with the plan. The other ladies were smiling, too.

"I can't force him," Camille protested. "If he doesn't want me—"

"Oh, please," B.J. said, irony lacing her words. "The man wants you so bad his tongue is hanging out. You just have to convince him his wants include marriage."

Camille wasn't sure she believed B.J. At least, she knew he wanted her in his bed. She just didn't know for how long.

But she wasn't going to go without trying one more time.

"All right."

"Great, come on." Megan grabbed her hand and pulled her out the door.

GRIFF WASN'T SLOW on the uptake. He knew what to do with a blanket spread over hay. All he had to do was get Camille to cooperate.

He spread the blanket carefully, then paced up and down the aisle between the horse stalls. What if Jake couldn't get her to come? What if she left before Jake found her? She seemed pretty upset to be discovered in his bed this morning.

Suddenly, he could wait no longer. He wasn't going to take a chance on her disappearing from his life. Not now that he'd found her, had discovered how important love and family could be.

He charged toward the barn door just as it opened.

Camille stepped inside, and the door behind her slammed shut.

Griff came to an abrupt halt.

Then they heard the door being barred.

Griff's gaze went from the door to Camille.

"Uh, Jake must not realize we're in here," he muttered, embarrassed now that he was a party to her being locked in.

"I'm sure he'll open it if you—"

"No!" He swallowed. "I mean, there's no hurry. I'd like to—to talk to you."

"I'm sorry about Mr. Haney. I know you didn't want to have to deal with your father." She took a step forward.

He remained where he was, afraid to come any closer until he knew he could touch her, hold her.

"I'll deal with it."

"You mean you aren't planning— I mean, are you still going to return to Chicago?"

Her blue eyes were huge, and he felt himself drowning in them. "Uh, that depends."

"On whether he'll leave you alone?" She took another step closer. "Is he unhappy that you're here?"

"No. No, he's happy. And he promised to not be a pest. He wanted to know me, but my mother refused. She lied to me, took money from him and kept us apart." His thoughts were on Camille, but some bitterness surged through his words.

She closed the distance between them, her hand reaching out to caress his cheek. "I'm so sorry."

His arms wrapped around her, bringing her irresistible body against his. It was her fault. She shouldn't have gotten so close.

"Camille—"

"Griff—" she said at the same time.

"Ladies first," he said as his hands rubbed her back, urging her closer.

"Last night, I said I understood that—that you didn't want marriage, family, but..." She paused and worried her bottom lip, and he thought he was going to die of hunger. "But I love you so much, and I insist that you tell me you don't want me. I'm not going to go away until you do." She squared her jaw and stared up at him, defiance in her every bone.

Griff realized then that he'd gotten lucky. So lucky he almost couldn't believe it. Not only had he found a family, a huge family of good people, but he'd also found a woman to love. A woman who loved him enough to fight for him.

"Well?" she asked softly, fear in her eyes.

"Sweetheart, I hope you brought all your belongings when you came here, because you're not ever going to get to leave."

He waited as his words sank into her. Then watched as her defiance turned into a happiness so bright he almost had to shield his eyes.

"You mean you want— I mean, you love me?"

"Of course I love you. I can't live without you. And I don't intend to. There's going to be another Randall wedding."

Their lips met, and that heady rush of feeling that always accompanied their embrace only increased as they professed their love.

"There's just one thing, sweetheart," Griff said as he pulled her with him to the nest he'd made in the hay.

"Yes?" she answered cautiously even as she sank down on the blanket with him.

"I think we're going to build our own house. I want to stay close to my cousins, but even you will have to admit that that house is full. Will you mind?"

"As long as we don't go too far away. I'll want some advice and support when we add to the Randall family."

He stared at her, and she asked anxiously, "You do want children, don't you?"

Pulling her against him, Griff gave thanks for all

the blessings he'd received since coming here. Maybe his mother had made up for her betrayal by sending him home to the Randalls.

"Oh, yeah," he assured Camille. "In fact, we can get started on them right now."

"WHAT DO YOU THINK they're doing?" Megan asked.

Chad put his arm around her. "What did we do in the barn?"

Her cheeks burned brightly, but she wasn't the only one to have sizzling memories tied to this building. B.J. in particular seemed to avoid everyone's stare.

They had gathered at the barn door just as Jake had locked it, all of them eager to know the outcome.

"Do you think they'll get married?" Toby asked.

"We're hoping so, son," Jake assured him. "We want both of them to hang around and be a part of the family."

"Well, when are they coming out?" the little boy asked.

"Um, sometimes these discussions take a long time," Jake assured him, and winked at B.J.

"But I didn't finish my breakfast."

"Come on, boy," Red said, extending a hand. "You and I and Mildred and the other kids will go back inside. It's cold out here, and we don't want any more sick ones."

The four couples looked at each other.

"Well," Pete said, "how long are we going to give them?"

"I think it's been long enough," Chad agreed.

Jake stepped up and pounded on the barn doors.

"Why doesn't he just open them?" Anna asked her husband.

Brett grinned. "'Cause the barn is kind of like that little old car that you were driving when we, uh, got together."

"Oh," she said, burying her face in his chest.

"Griff? You in there?"

"Dumb question, Jake. You locked the door on him," B.J. complained.

Before anyone else could say anything, they heard a faint response. "Go away!"

Megan stepped closer to the door. "Camille, are you okay?"

"Oh, yes" was the soft response.

"Are you two gonna get married?" Jake called.

"Yeah. Go away."

Everyone cheered. Then Jake called one last time, "We're serving champagne in the house...when you can get there."

There was no response.

Jake herded his family back to the house. "I think they're a little too busy to join us right now. But they'll eventually come out, I'm sure."

"Looks like our family is growing again," Pete said with satisfaction.

Epilogue

"Are you ready?" B.J. called into the bride's room at the church in Rawhide, where all the Randall wives but Megan had been married.

"Yes, I think— Oh, no!" Camille exclaimed as she grabbed her satin skirt and ran for the sink in the bathroom. The Randall women all looked at each other.

"Oh, my," Anna said softly, hurrying to support Camille.

"You didn't get it on your dress, did you?" Megan asked anxiously, trying to peer around Anna to check.

"I don't think so. I don't know what's wrong with me. I've been sick every morning for the past week, and I'm not the least bit nervous about marrying Griff," Camille said shakily. She came out of the bathroom and reached for the nearest chair.

"Crackers," B.J. said, causing Camille to stare at her, wondering if everyone had gone crazy.

"I'll get some," Janie said, though she wasn't sure where she'd find any.

"Check with Lindsey," Anna said. "She keeps them with her all the time." Lindsey was one of her patients.

"Why do you want crackers?" Camille asked.

"She doesn't know," B.J., Anna and Megan all said at once.

"What? It's probably just nerves. Though I don't understand—"

"Sweetie," Anna said softly, "I don't think you have to worry anymore about Griff being sterile."

"Oh, really? Doc said— Oh!" Camille exclaimed as she stared at the others. "You mean I'm pregnant?" There was wonder in her voice. She cradled her flat stomach, a smile building on her lips. "A baby."

"You'll have to get a blood test," Anna said, "but if I were you, I'd load up on crackers before you leave for your honeymoon."

Janie slipped back in and handed Camille some crackers.

As she began chewing one, a knock sounded on the door.

"What's taking you guys so long?" Chad demanded. "The bridegroom is about ready to come storming in here and claim his woman."

Camille stood. "My veil."

They all helped arrange the veil over her glossy blond curls, then stood back to admire her.

"You're a beautiful bride," Megan whispered. "Now we'll always be family."

Camille gave her a kiss on her cheek, then

stepped to the door, where Jake waited to give her away. She took his arm and smiled at him.

"Ready?" he whispered.

She nodded in return and watched Elizabeth and Caroline, in darling gold dresses, walk down the aisle together, dribbling rose petals. They stopped several times, especially when they discovered Doc sitting next to the aisle, but whoever was closest encouraged them to go on.

Since Camille wanted all the Randalls involved, even Torie went down the aisle, carried in her mother's arms. Brett was waiting for them near Griffin. Pete and Chad were there, too, and Toby, who was taking Jake's place.

When each of the Randall women had marched down the aisle, carrying an autumn arrangement against their golden taffeta gowns, meeting their escorts with sweet smiles at the altar, it was her turn.

She took Jake's arm, and started down the aisle, her gaze focused on her future husband. But she paused briefly as she passed Bill Haney.

The poor man had been so excited to be invited, he could hardly speak. She and Griff had talked a lot about Bill. Gradually her soon-to-be husband had accepted the man into his life.

Bill wanted to give them his ranch and move to Rawhide. Griff had offered to build another house for them on Bill's land, but Bill, finally realizing he wasn't going to be banished, took over the empty manager's house, redecorated by Megan and Camille. He seemed so happy now.

The past month had been frantic with all they had to do. It had been too long and too short. But it had been all the time Griff would permit. He wanted his bride.

And she wanted him, for the rest of her life.

When she reached his side, he took her hand in his. But Camille had a slight variation to make in the wedding ceremony. She tugged her hand free and lifted her veil, then put her arms around Griff's neck.

After a delicate whisper in his ear, Griffin Randall stared at his soon-to-be bride, lifted her against him and kissed her deeply.

The minister stared at the couple. "No, not yet! It's not time to kiss the bride yet!"

"Sorry, Pastor," Griff finally said after releasing a beaming Camille. "We can go ahead now."

Jake wasn't sure what the whispering and kissing had been about, but from the look on B.J.'s face, he figured it might be similar to the news his wife had given him a couple of days ago. The Randall family was going to be getting bigger than ever.

But he wasn't complaining. No, siree. Fortunately the Randall men, even Griff, had come to realize a great truth.

Never could have too much family.

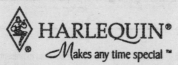

Take 2 bestselling love stories FREE

Plus get a FREE surprise gift!

Special Limited-Time Offer

Mail to Harlequin Reader Service®

3010 Walden Avenue
P.O. Box 1867
Buffalo, N.Y. 14240-1867

YES! Please send me 2 free Harlequin American Romance® novels and my free surprise gift. Then send me 4 brand-new novels every month, which I will receive months before they appear in bookstores. Bill me at the low price of $3.34 each plus 25¢ delivery and applicable sales tax, if any.* That's the complete price, and a saving of over 10% off the cover prices—quite a bargain! I understand that accepting the books and gift places me under no obligation ever to buy any books. I can always return a shipment and cancel at any time. Even if I never buy another book from Harlequin, the 2 free books and the surprise gift are mine to keep forever.

154 HEN CH7E

Name _____ (PLEASE PRINT)

Address _____ Apt. No. _____

City _____ State _____ Zip _____

This offer is limited to one order per household and not valid to present Harlequin American Romance® subscribers. *Terms and prices are subject to change without notice. Sales tax applicable in N.Y.

UAMER-98   ©1990 Harlequin Enterprises Limited

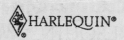

Not The Same Old Story!

 Exciting, glamorous romance stories that take readers around the world.

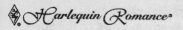 Sparkling, fresh and tender love stories that bring you pure romance.

 Bold and adventurous— Temptation is strong women, bad boys, great sex!

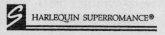 Provocative and realistic stories that celebrate life and love.

 Contemporary fairy tales—where anything is possible and where dreams come true.

 Heart-stopping, suspenseful adventures that combine the best of romance and mystery.

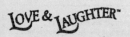 Humorous and romantic stories that capture the lighter side of love.

Look us up on-line at: http://www.romance.net   HGENERIC

Catch more great

HARLEQUIN™ **Movies**

featured on the movie channel tmc

Premiering September 12th
A Change of Place
Starring Rick Springfield and
Stephanie Beacham. Based on the novel
by bestselling author Tracy Sinclair

Don't miss next month's movie!
Premiering October 10th
Loving Evangeline
Based on the novel by *New York Times*
bestselling author Linda Howard

If you are not currently a subscriber to
The Movie Channel, simply call your
local cable or satellite provider for more
details. Call today, and don't miss out
on the romance!

the movie channel tmc   HARLEQUIN®

100% pure movies.   *Makes any time special* ™
100% pure fun.

An Alliance Television Production

HARLEQUIN®
AMERICAN ◆ ROMANCE®

*Under an assumed name, a woman delivers
twins at Oregon's Valley Memorial
Hospital, only to disappear...leaving
behind the cooing twin girls and a note
listing their dad as D. K. McKeon. Only
trouble is, there are three D. K. McKeons....*

So the question is

**WHO'S THE
DADDY?**

Muriel Jensen
brings you a delightfully funny trilogy of
one mystery, two gurgling babies and
three possible daddies!

Don't miss:

#737 DADDY BY DEFAULT
(August 1998)

#742 DADDY BY DESIGN
(September 1998)

#746 DADDY BY DESTINY
(October 1998)

HARLEQUIN®
Makes any time special ™

MEN at WORK

All work and no play?
Not these men!

July 1998
MACKENZIE'S LADY by Dallas Schulze

Undercover agent Mackenzie Donahue's
lazy smile and deep blue eyes were his best
weapons. But after rescuing—and kissing!—
damsel in distress Holly Reynolds, how could
he betray her by spying on her brother?

MEN
IN
UNIFORM

August 1998
MISS LIZ'S PASSION by Sherryl Woods

Todd Lewis could put up a building with ease,
but quailed at the sight of a classroom! Still,
Liz Gentry, his son's teacher, was no battle-ax,
and soon Todd started planning some
extracurricular activities of his own....

MEN of STEEL

September 1998
A CLASSIC ENCOUNTER
by Emilie Richards

Doctor Chris Matthews was intelligent, sexy
and *very* good with his hands—which made
him all the more dangerous to single mom
Lizette St. Hilaire. So how long could she
resist Chris's special brand of TLC?

DOCTOR, DOCTOR

Available at your favorite retail outlet!

MEN AT WORK™

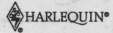

HARLEQUIN®   Silhouette®

Look us up on-line at: http://www.romance.net   PMAW2

SEXY, POWERFUL MEN NEED EXTRAORDINARY WOMEN WHEN THEY'RE

Destined for Love

Take a walk on the wild side this October
when three bestselling authors weave wondrous stories
about heroines who use their extraspecial abilities to
achieve the magic and wonder of love!

HATFIELD AND McCOY
by HEATHER GRAHAM POZZESSERE

LIGHTNING STRIKES
by KATHLEEN KORBEL

MYSTERY LOVER
by ANNETTE BROADRICK

Available October 1998
wherever Harlequin and Silhouette books are sold.

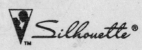

Intense, dazzling, isolated...

THE

AUSTRALIANS

Stories of romance Australian-style, guaranteed to
fulfill that sense of adventure!

This October, look for

Beguiled and Bedazzled
by **Victoria Gordon**

Colleen Ferrar is a woman who always gets what she wants—
that is, until she meets Devon Burns, who lives in the very
secluded Tasmanian bush. He has a proposal of his own, and
the question is: how far will Colleen go to get what she wants?

*The Wonder from Down Under: where spirited women win
the hearts of Australia's most independent men!*

Available October 1998
at your favorite retail outlet.

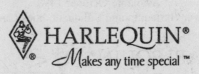

HARLEQUIN®
Makes any time special ™